Mark

Shaun Levin

ALSO BY SHAUN LEVIN

Alone with a Man in a Room

Seven Sweet Things

Snapshots of The Boy

A Year of Two Summers

Isaac Rosenberg's Journey to Arras

Trees at a Sanatorium

Mark

Treehouse Press, 2021

This is a work of fiction

Parts of this book have been published in different form as "Hope, or: The Beginning of Love" in *Litro Magazine* (86, 2006), as "Mark Gertler in 13 Sketches" in *Moment Magazine* (2007), and as *Trees at a Sanatorium* (Sylph Editions, 2011).

cover: detail from Mark Gertler "The Artist in His Studio" courtesy of Piano Nobile, Robert Travers (Works of Art) Ltd.

A catalogue record of this book is available from the British Library.

ISBN: 978-0-9563775-8-6

"Next time you want to unpack your heart,
don't do it before a realistic writer."

*letter from William Rothenstein
to Mark Gertler (4 July 1918)*

Acknowledgments

For their company and help, either or both, I am deeply grateful to Beldan Sezen, and to Geof Dalton, Simon Tabak, Maggie Hamand, Sarah Salway, Linsey Robin, Georgina Denn, Joel Bevin, Sarah MacDougall, Rachel Dickson, Luke Gertler, Frances Guilfoyle, Alex Robertson, Colin Manning, Kerstin Hoge, and Robert Travers.

Thanks to Arts Council England, Hawthornden Literary Retreat, the City of Hobart and the Tasmanian Writers Centre, Fundación Valparaíso in Spain, and the Bundanon Trust in Australia for the gift of time and space to write.

Madrid, 2021

Contents

Part 1

Part 2

Part 1

Spain

❧

I

■ After the rain had stopped we left the Jewish Quarter and headed towards the café on Plaça de la Independència for *xocolata* and *xurros*, those crusty worm-like donuts dipped into muddy chocolate. We'd spent the morning in the Museum on Carrer Sant Llorenç in the *Call Jueu* in Girona wrapped in a delicious kind of diasporic sadness, two Jews where once there'd been many. *When the Jews left Girona*, the guide tells us, as if they'd decided, okay, enough's enough, packed their bags, and headed off, as if history is simply a series of choices, *they went to Amsterdam, France, North Africa*. Gabriel had pressed against me – he could tell I was about to say something that might embarrass him (I'd done it before).

We were on our way to Barcelona, a kind of holiday, but for me, another stop on a research journey in the footsteps of Mark Gertler, a British painter who'd killed

1

himself in 1939. I'd grown tired of writing my own story, bored with the repetition of the "I," "my" and "me" of childhood and adolescence. Enough already. I wanted someone else's life to write about. A couple of years ago, at Leeds Art Gallery on my way back to London from a writing retreat in Yorkshire, I'd encountered Mark Gertler's *Pond at Garsington*. Something about the intense melancholy of its greens and browns, colours I'd never seen in English painting, had set me off on this exploration. For a long time, I'd been drawn to painting as a way into words, and now here he was, a Jewish painter in England, linked to the Bloomsbury crowd, so beautiful, too, and I felt that I may have found my subject, a way out of myself.

The guide in Girona tells us that the Ramban lived here, that this was the birthplace of the Kabbalah. "It's hard to be certain about these things," I say to Gabriel afterwards, "when our people keep moving around so much." We're sitting in the museum's glass-fronted room looking out onto the courtyard, a marble Magen David set into its terracotta tiles, a gesture of permanence for what is no longer here. A rose bush arches across the entrance, an explosion of pink petals like Love Hearts. Rain slides from the leaves of an orange tree, a lemon tree, the thick corrugated leaves of a loquat tree, and every fifteen minutes cathedral bells fill the space with their clang of imminent doom.

How did the Jews live in the shadow of such a building? And these riches? A synagogue that no longer exists, boys spying on the bishops, longing for altar boys – who amongst *them* is our ancestor?

Gabriel orders *xurros* and *xocolata* for both of us.

"I like it when you order in Spanish," I say.

"You'll do the same when we go to Israel," he says.

"I like my lovers to know things I don't."

"You're avoiding the issue."

"Trust me," I say, "you don't want to go there. I've got a better idea. Draw me while we wait for the chocolate. Draw me and tell me what's going through your head. I want to know how an artist thinks."

"I can't do that," he says, his eyes darting between my face and his sketchbook. "I need to concentrate. I can't do two things at once."

"Try," I say.

"You always want me to talk," he says. "*You* talk."

"About what?"

"I don't know," he says.

"I've got nothing to say."

"Then talk about me," he says. "Put me into words."

"You're lovely to kiss," I say. "Did you know that? I was thinking about that this morning. Your lips, the blush and rose of your cheeks. Is that what you want to hear?"

"Shut up and keep talking," he says.

"You have the loveliest back to stroke, long and smooth, and the soft hairs at the base that lead to the glen between your arse-cheeks, so wonderful to lick, and that grand *schwanz*, what an honour, and what a fine body to hold – so slim and firm, so elegant – and a face! That *ponim*. To gaze upon that *scheine ponim*, so open, so loving, and those eyes, *kein ayin hora*, so green, the rarest of all colours."

We could be anywhere: back at the hotel, at home in our bed, in my flat, at his, as if nobody was anywhere near us and we're alone in the woods, on a mountain, walking by a stream, naked on a beach, the sun at high noon, cocooned in the heat, wrapped in our sleeping bags on the slopes of Mount Kilimanjaro.

"How am I doing?" I say.

"Where have you been all my life?" he says.

There are too many things that cannot be voiced, too much has happened that must be kept from you, which is why I'm heading to Sitges on my own, the town Gertler visited with his wife and some friends back in 1917, hoping to have a word with Picasso.

"While I'm in Sitges," I say. "You must paint."

"It's not that easy," he says.

"This is good," I say, about to dive in with another finger of *xurros*.

■ Snow had been falling all afternoon, masses of thick

clouds releasing their flakes quietly, the way snow is gentle and soft, and the flakes trickle down, puffed-up, gathering on the ground, clinging to branches and gas lamps. Snow gathers on the shoulders of the porter carrying Gertler's suitcases up to the entrance, stamping his feet on the doormat to clear his boots. As if the whole thing, Gertler thinks, is just a skiing holiday or the beginning of an excursion to the South of France. *Allons-y*. As if none of this is the result of a slow wasting away, lungs failing, blood coughed up into his mouth then spat out. It's the greatest crisis of his life, here at the sanatorium in Banchory.

■ We're naked in our hotel room. Impromptu *shabbes* candles on the dressing table, left-over chicken bones and broccoli stems on the plates on the floor, and Gabriel asks to slow down our lovemaking. That's what he calls it: Making love. And me, I just want the fucking that comes at the beginning, the urgent storytelling, a ferocious hunger to be consumed and known. I want the fidelity at the beginning of love.

"I've never met anyone like you," he says. "I feel wrapped in kisses."

■ He thinks of his mother in the dark kitchen of the house on Spital Square, the chill of winter threatening from outside, the noise of street hawkers, a tunnel of weak light, sliced on all corners by the window frame. He sees a table with tulips, a guitar, the door flung open and there she is, weighed down by baskets: cabbages, carrots, greens and oranges, beetroot in browns and purples. Earthy mushrooms, parsnips. Through the window, a chimney puffs its smoke against luminous grey, flecks of pink across the sky. While his mother catches her breath, he sketches her at the table, hands of clay – a large woman, flesh and greenery in the warm dark kitchen. And in the yard below, a neighbour hangs her washing: white knickers, blue shirts, bright green skirt, the sky pink, the light in the oblong windows – the palest of lemon. He sits content, caring for no person or nothing, relishing the horrible loneliness and isolation that brings pain and meaning to his life.

"Mr Gertler," the nurse interrupts. "It's time for dinner."

It was at that moment, the moment he'll remember all his life, that he knew his one wish, the feat that would justify his existence, as he lay in the white room wrapped in the sanatorium's white sheets, the night air drifting in through the window, that his single purpose was to make paintings of great beauty, barbaric in their realism, beauty trembling on the edges of dread.

"It's fish," the nurse says.

"Yes," he says, turning away.

Thinking: *Shabbes*.

No one had ever seemed more beautiful and essential to him than Carrington. His body craves hers, he's walking in the dark with no candles to light the way. At dinner, his food will sit untouched, the pastry crust thin, the colour of sea-sand, brown at the rim, a roof to the chunks of cod and white sauce, buttressed by small mounds of peas and carrots. Eventually he will bite: the fish will be soft, the pastry crust will be soft, everything will melt in his mouth.

There are moments, even though his lungs are collapsing, his chest weak, when he comforts himself with thoughts of slicing his own throat.

As if he'd known word was on its way, a note arrives at the sanatorium: the rosy-cheeked maid brings it to his table. Even if it's just a brief note, he can barely eat his dinner, and he continues to shake all night. He'd imagined a resentment on her part, a *broigez*, that she'd thought he'd been indiscreet, because he'd told the Garsington lot what had happened between them. He begins to compose a letter. *You will always mean something special to me. I have felt hurt at your silence.* They must have told her that a few weeks ago at Ottoline's on Gower Street he'd begun to cough up blood, morsels of his own raw lungs.

With the blood came the realisation that he'd be banished to a place like this. As if that wasn't enough, Marchant had gone and died. They'd had an arrangement, a contract promising him a stipend of £35 a month whether he sold paintings or not. Now he doubted the gallery would honour its promise. *But believe me,* he continued his letter to Carrington, *I appreciate your little note. It has made me happy, even if I do feel a hundred years old.*

■ What I don't say is: I will always avoid the happiness that lasts from one day to the next, night to night. Don't talk to me daily of the same things in the same tone of voice, it brings out the ferocity in me. Give me the kind of man who, like the sun in this part of the world (England), does not appear every day.

"You're so hard on yourself," Gabriel says.

"And you're not?" I say.

"Not now," he says. "Not when I'm with you."

"So," I say, getting up to sit on the edge of the bed. "Are we going out? There's the Picasso Museum to see."

"We need to stretch first," he says.

Moving together through the sun salutation, I'm surprised how much I remember from those yoga classes at Tel Aviv University when a group of us gathered once a week in a hall in the basement of the student dorms, an instructor trying her best to get us all to relax. I turn to watch Gabriel stretch. He knows I'm looking but stares straight ahead to keep his balance, just a smile appearing, the smile of the appreciated, a little-boy kind of smile. His long body, its taste a reminder of some Israeli men

I've known, Moroccan men in particular, as if the sun has left its mark on his skin, and the firmness of youth, skin close to muscle, the furrow down the centre of his back.

"What's that between your legs?" he says.

"I'm stretching," I say. "All of me is stretching."

"Punch me in the mouth," I say.

"Stop it," he says.

"Slap me," I say. "Here."

When he'd said the three words to me the night before, the I and love and you words, my heart had tightened. What I don't say to him is that it's not just about shame, the psyche is more complicated than that. And I wonder: Would I have felt differently if I'd been the one doing the fucking, and hadn't been so quick to sit on him while we played with Spanish phrases, pretending to be actors in a Mexican soap opera: *Mi amor*, he says, and I repeat after him, him inside me. *Te amo mas que a mi vida*, we say. And: *nunca te dejaré*. And once more with feeling, like we really mean it.

■ Not a single night's rest in all the eight days he's been here. Fits and starts and being woken by coughing, his own or someone else's, slime, mucous, the hawking up of sputum. He dreams of wolves and bears on the icy plains of Siberia, being dragged back in time, his ancestors growing out of peasanthood into what? Something better? With enough money to leave Przemsyl and trek to London. In the dream, the gardener at the sanatorium, in military uniform, helping Gertler into a carriage drawn by skinny horses, plodding through the village after dark, windows illuminated. In the dream, it's midnight, though he tells himself it must be dawn, it must be morning. The only sound is the clop clop of hooves on cobblestones, and the light and the waking and the soft rasping of Julian's knuckles on his bedroom door.

"I'm so grateful to see you."

"What were you dreaming?" she says, putting a glass of milk at his bedside. So pretty (so unlike her mother), uninhibited (so like her mother): it was madness on Ottoline's part to let her play naked by the pond, making it even harder for Gertler to look at her now.

"They should put a sign around your neck," he says.

"Saying what?" she says, opening the curtains and plonking herself down on the window seat.

"Something like: Don't forget I am only fourteen."

He lifts his head off the pillow and drinks his milk in three gulps. He puts the glass back and makes a gesture across his chest to indicate a large placard. And she laughs, throwing her head back. To make him look? Her neck. What's a fourteen year old girl supposed to say to a twenty-nine year old man?

"Will you wait for me downstairs?" he says – then

does the unthinkable. Sees her coming back from tennis, walking through the orchard, sweat coating her, making her slippery. He watches through the holes in the shrubbery, his vision blurred and sharpened by desire, her skin browned by the sun, short skirt and singlet, sweat running down her belly, gathering in a pool, the image enlarged to fill the canvas, her naked body before him. And he kneels, his face between her legs, lapping at her like a cat, a dog, a wolf: crazed with thirst and shame. So soft and smooth, her little breasts, her skin, the V. She holds the back of his head and pulls him into her, harder and harder until he is swallowed whole.

"Are you awake, Mr Gertler?"

He smiles faintly at the nurse, blinks to indicate that, yes, he is wide awake.

"A restless night?" the nurse says.

"May I have some milk?" he says.

"It's there," she says, pointing.

When she leaves, he ejaculates sticky lumps into an old handkerchief, and there is guilt, pure sweet guilt, his desire's intensity surprising him. Eventhough it was only a dream, eventhough Ottoline's daughter is no longer fourteen, every time he sees Julian he will have a moment of blushing. The divide between not doing and grabbing, the way Carrington had claimed he'd done to her, forced himself on her, such a thin *mechitza* between thought and action. The image of her fades, of Julian, of

Carrington, as if he is gazing at them through the wrong end of a telescope.

■ The men around us were all high on poppers. At some point we'd moved away from the crowd and gone to sit in a corner of the steam room, taking it in turns to rest against each other's body. On the periphery, two men in towels from their waists to their ankles floated across the terracotta floor like mermaids, any minute now and they'd break into a number from *Splash* or *South Pacific*. Four men moving as an ensemble, three dark-skinned, bodies identical, and a taller, stockier light-skinned American with a towel up to his armpits, a particularly large towel, which made me wonder if some men brought their own towels from home.

"It's been a while since I've had sex with someome so intelligent," I said.

"Have we had sex already?" Gabriel said.

"Not yet," I said.

"I'm not usually attracted to intelligent men," he said.

"Oh, good," I said, "because I'm not."

Now I sit in the hotel bar while Gabriel is upstairs taking a mid-morning nap. Who is he, this man I've brought along with me on my wild goose chase. I want to go up and wake him and say: *I don't deserve someone like you.*

I've been walking around for too long without a "we" or "us" in my lexicon. You have no idea how terrified I am. But I wait in the bar, and while I wait, I read from Gertler's letters, one of them to Nevinson: *We are destined to be rivals and rivals we must remain, openly, dramatically, theatrically. Not friends. I am sorry, but that is how it must be.*

On our way through the market off Las Ramblas, we stop at a cheese stand to buy manchego cheese, then a couple of bright pink pitango fruit, a slab of fig cake. At the other end of the market, Gabriel shows me the art school he went to when he'd followed a girlfriend to Barcelona and landed up staying to study painting. We sit by the fountain in the courtyard surrounded by two buildings, the Biblioteca de Catalunya and his school, tall orange trees heavy with fruit all around us. We eat from the fig cake he was planning to offer friends in his life-drawing group back in London, then we head to La Gardunya for lunch, the café he used to come to after classes.

Paella mixta with crabs, prawns, langoustine and chunks of squid, mussels in their shells – all tinted and perfumed with saffron. All unkosher. *Treif.* But Gabriel reassures me he *wants* to eat them, says my excitement is contagious. The background music is Cassandra Wilson, her mournful, crisp rendition of "Tupelo Honey." A table of Catalans, three men and two women, loud and gesticulating, discussing something of consequence (politics? sex?), all of them with cigarettes. An older woman eats at a small table on her own, sucking the flesh out of clam shells, chewing on calamari, not wiping her hands and mouth until she is finished.

For dessert: *arroz con leche*, a rice pudding with sugar and cinnamon – each grain distinguishable. The waiter and I flirt with each other. Betrayal's an exciting option. I am a toxic audience when it comes to telling me your stories. You'd be so easy to hurt, I think.

"He was working here back then, too," Gabriel says.

"Does he remember you?" I say.

"No," he say. "But he seems to remember *you*."

■ Because Gertler had finally popped the question: "Would you like to have sex one day?" And Carrington had said: "Is that a…" And Gertler had said: "Because I think about it all the time." And she'd said: "I think about it, too. I've thought about it a lot, but it would have to be the right time and the right situation. It couldn't be a planned thing. We'd have to do it not for other people."

People had been talking, asking questions, expecting them to, so they tried and failed and now they're silent, Gertler naked on the bed, arms across his chest. In the chill of the room, the warmth of Carrington's body from where she sits at the foot of the bed, hugging her knees as if holding a baby.

"I couldn't breathe," she says.

She doesn't want him pushing against her, his face on hers, so close, an attack, like an animal licking her lips. Yet his body is so delicate, so tender, she never has to censor herself with him, to explain things. But his hunger tests her integrity. At least Lytton would never love her enough to make demands, her adoration for him would nourish them both. Gertler threatened to disrupt her fragile self, the brittle sense of separateness from her family. When he's on top of her, she freezes, her body paralysed. One minute she's excited, like she could make love forever, then a single wrong gesture, a kiss that lasts too long, a lizard tongue in her mouth, and she freezes.

"Tell me what's going on inside you," he says.

"Don't ask me to talk about my inner self," she says.

On the edge of his bed in the sanatorium willing himself to stand, to move towards the easel set up in this grand prison of boredom. He hears her breathing, slow and controlled, withdrawing, guilty for turning away – *is there something wrong with me?* – and all she really wants is for him to know her completely.

"I feel ashamed and unclean," she says.

"How can you say that? My desire is beautiful."

"But your body," she says. "I don't want a body pressing into me."

"You said I was beautiful. You called me pretty."

"But this," she says, her hand moving down his

stomach, so smooth and soft, like her own, stopping at the top of his pubic hair: black and silky.

"My pork sausage?" he says.

"Why can't it be like at the mill? You were splendid then, all week."

"You said 'I'm happy when you love me'."

"I am," she said. "You're such a good comrade."

"But I want more," he said. "Just as painting is an expression of art, fucking expresses love. You can't have them separately. Then you're just a crap artist, like... like... you know who, people like him express nothing but their own stupidity."

Her back an invitation and rejection, neck exposed, her hair in a bob. From behind, they look like twins.

■ Soon after the Catalans conquered Sardinia in 990 they built the church of Santa Maria del Mar, the first thing the sailors would see when they sailed back into Barcelona, a place to give thanks to the Virgin for keeping them afloat. During the Spanish Civil War, the church was gutted and ransacked. It smells now of fresh cement and burning candles. We walk through it holding hands, then down to the beach and along the shore, the sand grainy, unrefined, the warm winter sun on our faces, on everything, and I think how ambling along a boardwalk hand-in-hand makes you part of normal human behaviour, that you and everyone else are the same: I belong to someone, and because of that, I belong. Or maybe this is what happens when you're so close to any great force of nature and all human life – the pettiness of fears and mistrust and bigotry – is rendered miniscule, even silly.

It's enough to make one happy.

While we walk up Carrer de la Marina, past the bullring and towards La Sagrada Famillia, Gabriel tells me how his mother used to lock him in his room when he was a child. It's a story he tells to explain the genesis of his desire to paint. His dad was a doctor, his mother – a socialist, brought up amongst the Jews of Leeds (her father had known Jacob Kramer). Locked in his room, Gabriel would pile his text books on his desk, take out a blank sheet of paper, and draw with coloured pencils, the same picture, over and over, always delicate creepers growing up Doric columns, tiny purple flowers, leaves shaped like raindrops. He imagined living in the large houses he drew, vast rooms to himself, no need for friends or his mother, and every time he drew that house, he drew himself in it, barefoot on the marble floors, leaning against the front wall, hidden behind a column, looking out onto the garden. Then he'd finish his homework, always neat and correct.

■ Some patients are well enough to travel home for Christmas.

Bye.

Bye.

Gertler's show at the Goupil opens in two months. Still a few pictures to do for Carrington: the apple-faced maid with the vermillion cheeks, the handsome medical student, a landscape he's working on: *Trees at a Sanatorium*. Earlier, the Jewish Mr Brahms had tried to rope him into a game of golf with him and his wife (she was lodging at a B&B in the village). They are dull and stupid, loud and offensive, and they think there's a natural bond between them. Despite the fact, he writes to Carrington, that they've never even heard of Renoir.

But they've been to Italy.

"Yes," Mr Brahms says. "Those wonderful Italians."

"Dear old Giotto," the wife exclaims (apropos of nothing).

The words keep ringing in Gertler's ears all day, and whenever he sees them, spies them at lunch, then at tea time, then dinner, the phrases come back to him:

Those wonderful Italians.

Dear old Giotto.

The Brahmses had introduced him to an American poet who insisted on reading her poems to everyone, making sure Mrs Brahms heard them, too, before she went back to her lodgings.

"My Lord," said Mr Brahms. "How do you do it?"

"They just come to me," the poet said.

She had the air of a novelist about her. She made

him think of Lytton, of Virginia. You're only angry at yourself, he thinks. Leave the poor poet alone. Or a bit like Eddie when he's tipsy. She liked an audience. He should have said to her (but, really, there was no one here worth opening one's mouth for): Go deeper. Bring your history to the poems, bring your core. It's what he's been trying to do ever since *Merry-Go-Round*.

Now at the window of his room, the night air sharp and cold, paint drying on the canvas, he reminds himself not to get entangled in the drama of these people. The work is what matters, getting this landscape done for the show. The room at night with its windows open to the darkness, and those wonderful Italians!

■ Painters seem happy to work together in a studio, paint outdoors in a group, let others peek over their shoulders. I've tried to be like that as I follow Gertler to places he went to, hauling my notebook out of the confines of my hovel to create in full view of the world. I want a communal writing table, to sit in art galleries and cafés and public parks, notebook on lap. I've always been a writer-scavenger, the magpie type, the kind who goes after things that sparkle, reads books, goes to exhibitions, the theatre, has friends, relations, takes the shiny bits, drags the glitter and tinsel back to his hell, I mean cell. When you write, you are abandoned, flung out to fend for yourself. But you are also the maker of destinies, the scribe, the tribe's narrator, the one relied on for story-feeding.

I don't want to approach the page empty-handed, and by empty-handed I mean with no hand in mine. Mark Gertler is my attempt at a different angle on my own story. We come from the same gene pool: Eastern European Jews escaping poverty and pogroms. There's no glory in our past. No glory besides survival.

■ The next morning, Gabriel is showering before his train to the airport, and the news comes through about Israel shelling Gaza City. Hamas had been firing rockets into Sderot and Ashkelon, and now Israel's doing its thing: making incursions into Palestinian territory, amassing forces on the border, calling up reservists. I am grateful to be on my own when they mention the war, glad that Gabriel is not witnessing what's happening. As if I'd never left. As if I'm trapped again. As if I could forget what I'd seen, the shame go away, as if distance and time could erase anything. Just when you're beginning to think ignoring it can make it go away, just when you're starting to feel they can't do that to you again, that a truce is the beginning of peace, an end to violence… you're back at square one.

I'm there at the shower when Gabriel is ready to step out (a church steeple in the sun, a heart that is a lake, boundless), but I step towards him and we stand under the water together, one of us about to leave, one just beginning, the warm water cocooning us. We hold each other – me I hold him, I hold him more – our bodies clinging and slippery. We kiss under the shower's stream, but it's awkward and water gets in our noses and we cough and splutter and laugh and he says let's get out, I have a flight to catch.

The sadness is not for me, not for what I've seen and done – that cannot be undone – but for the young men being forced to do what I did, go where I went, witness what I saw, worse (war gets crueller each time), for the people they will kill, for a nation with a centuries-old death-wish.

"Are you okay?" Gabriel says when I'm back in the room, a towel around my waist, not unaware of his appreciation – he's told me this – of me naked in a towel, for this is how we'd met, and you in a towel, he'd said, is a sight for sore eyes.

"Did you hear the news?" I say.

"They had it coming," he says.

"Don't talk like that."

"What's up?' he says.

I dry myself with the towel, help him button his shirt, straighten his collar.

"I can stay," he says.

"It's just a bit of research," I say. "I'll be home soon."

"You really are," he says, and steps back to look, "a

sight for sore eyes."

"Stop."

"Make me," he says.

I keep my eyes on his, even while he lifts his hand to my face, to hold my cheek against his open palm, warm and dry and smelling of lavender soap. We lean into each other and kiss and it's like a shudder, a premonition. His kiss is everything: home and God and family and desire and safety and all questions answered, the full stop to stop all doubt. If I were to pray it would be *Shema Yisrael*, not because we are soon to plunge swords into our hearts before the Romans get here, but because it is morning and we have risen and it is a new day.

II

■ Gertler met the Swedish painter in the room down the corridor, a man with strands of hair hanging off his scalp like a cape. The man was sick of doing abstract work, so he'd turned to nature for its chaos and harmony.

"I am not any more interested in feelings," the Swede had said. "Enough of that vomit."

Gertler isn't allowed out, but the Swede heads to the woods every day, crawls up and down the hill to work on his paintings. He's good enough company, but a poor listener and as far as Gertler can tell, too afraid to create his own painterly language: the colours are strong, the images are precise, but there is nothing of him in them. *All well and good to say I see this before me*, Gertler writes to Carrington, *but you have to find a way to make the landscape yours.*

Dr Lucas had promised a high stool to raise him to the level of the subject he wants to work on: the trees on the other side of the lawn. It has taken him a while to get used to this room and to think of it as a studio. He starts with a few sketches, hides them between the pages of the Goya book. He reminds himself to let the space and light dictate the work, just as if this was Garsington. The winter sun is everywhere, and from the window he watches the leaves, light shining through them, turning them to lace. "Just remember," the doctor keeps saying. "You're here for your health." But whenever he comes into the room he's always asking, "Done any sketching yet?"

It's mid-December, and the mountains are the browns and russet golds of the Old Masters – some are cobalt blue, the magenta of Matisse. The snow caps are white against white, tinted with aquamarine.

In a smaller room on the floor below, a handsome young student likes to draw, so Gertler persuades him to buy a set of oils. He's helping him with a self-portrait. In a letter to Carrington, he promises to send a picture of the young man, says they've been discussing "a sense of painting" – that awareness of the craft and the place one reaches through constant work and experimentation and error – and about what it takes to paint the kind of painting that makes one say: "Ah, that is lovely stuff."

On Gertler's birthday, the student's brother picks them up and they head to Aberdeen for a little celebration. The Swedish painter joins them, and a tailor from Lanarkshire – one of the most loveable people I've ever met, he tells Carrington. They drink wine and port and liqueurs and eat mince pies and smoke cigars, and Gertler basks in the warmth of the restaurant, thinks of Thursdays when friends would come for his regular "at homes" and of the first time Ottoline visited, Lady Ottoline Morrell striding down Bishopsgate towards his studio. It was as if that moment in Aberdeen could have happened at any time of year – maybe this wasn't the middle of winter – and they were there with their ties undone, shirts unbuttoned, laughing at Gertler's perfect imitation of Mr Brahms and his wife: "Oh, those lovely Italians!"

■ At the adjacent table, a woman wraps a couple of pastries in napkins while her children watch. At another, a mother, daughter and grandparents sit in silence. The mother strokes her daughter's cheek, then lowers her hand to rest on her daughter's arm. At the table next to theirs, a guy chats to a woman in a mauve jumper. They speak with animated gestures, the man puts his fingers over his eyes to indicate the cool shades he saw someone wearing. They laugh a lot, touch, enjoy the feel of each other's skin under their fingertips.

Three young girls drink tea. An old man drinks hot chocolate and smokes a cigarillo. Lovers occupy the tables in the centre of the café. The women cling to their men, and the men, lounging in their chairs, cling back with a half-Nelson. A couple outside on the pavement sit on a motorbike, each resting a foot on the railings, she in a red jumper and turquoise shoes, he in tracksuit bottoms tucked into pink socks. Their hair is curly, down to their shoulders, and they smile at each other as if they could disappear into each other's mouths, as if love were a happy carnivore. I'd be the same if Gabriel was here, I'd want the world to see what's happening between us. In my plan for the future, we're on holiday together, spending our days writing and painting and when evening comes, we meet for burgers and go in and out of small-talk and feed each other fries and look at the sea with our arms around each other and say things like: *Mi amor, no puedo vivir sin ti.*

■ Mahmoud Ahmadinejad says Israel has pressed its self-destruct button. The Israeli ambassador to the UN, Dan Gillerman, seems genuinely scared of the Iranian President and urges the world to take note of what the man is saying, as if to say: You were silent when Hitler did what he did, make sure you don't stand and watch again. The news returns to Gaza, back to smoke rising from the buildings, the sound of rockets, back to human shields, to collateral damage, to the keeping score of dead bodies, to the caution and smoke-screen of language. I don't want to be alone in my room.

■ Mauro is an Argentinean with dreadlocks and he's into grunge, so I get extra points for being from Israel – he's a fan of some grunge band from Haifa. (What's grunge? But I don't ask.) I want to be close to him, listen to everything he has to say as if hidden treasures nestled on his skin, in his mouth. I will tolerate a great deal for the sake of beauty: boredom, repetition, hesitation, torture, deviation, devise endless questions to demonstrate fascination, all just to be close to men like him. I'm so caught up in Mauro's beauty I can't tell whether he's flirting or just working for his tip. As if I didn't have a man waiting for me at home, as if I hadn't been thinking that Gabriel might be The One.

"Foreigners in Sitges," Mauro says. "We have to stick together. Catalans don't want us."

Apparently the bohemians in town are all South America artists and musicians. Mauro tells me that this is the gay capital of Spain. *Nah! Really?* And for the few days I'm in Sitges, he is on breakfast duty in the hotel dining room. He is the first man I see every morning. My

26

first words of the day are to him.

■ Gertler painted for an hour by the window, then retreated to bed, colours still wet on his fingers, to sleep in his own mess, as if the bed-linen were more canvas, shapes forming on sheets and pillows while he naps, then waking again with the sun high in the sky. Later that afternoon they'll sit in a café on Passeig de la Ribera – him and Marjorie and her dreaded friend Greville – and they'll observe. Gertler will sketch. Marjorie will eat bread with crushed tomato and olive oil.

"Does anyone know those two gentlemen?" Gertler will say.

Two barefooted Englishmen at the table next to theirs, both in white cotton shirts. They seem at home here, sitting with their faces turned to the afternoon sun, one with a manicured beard, the other with the kind of fair-haired floppy fringe that reminds Gertler of Garsington, of Huxley and Sassoon, all of them posing on the lawn.

"Talk to them," Greville says. "They look like fun."

Gertler will wait and see what the couple do, perhaps they'll do or say the kind of outrageous thing that always lifts his spirits. They touch each other when they talk, the bearded one resting his hand on the other's knee, then they each take out a notebook – one to sketch, the other to write – and they are as good as gone. Every so often, the bearded one puts his hand into a small paper bag and feeds himself and his lover strips of orange rind coated in chocolate.

"Okay," says Greville. "I'm ready for my main course."

"Yes," Marjorie says. "More food is needed."

The waiter brings out plates of noodles with a dollop of red sauce. Gertler enjoys slurping noodles into his mouth, like some *vilde chaya*. What he cannot see yet is the way Marjorie is moving between nausea and savage hunger, she could devour the entire table in a single gulp. The only way to get rid of the bitter taste is to keep eating, keep chewing and swallowing while the child inside her keeps growing.

Greville's bright idea is that they go skinny-dipping on the other side of the church, but Gertler is quite happy to stay here till evening and slurp worms into his mouth. The sound and mess are soothing – he's a baby bird in a nest. When Greville and Marjorie leave, the spaghetti-worms begin to move across the table, snake their way across the surface, slip off the table and into his lap, up his arms, down his legs, winding themselves around his wrists and ankles like shackles and bracelets, strips of red across his flesh. At this time of day – sunset just before 6pm – the blue turns to aquamarine, the world is lapis lazuli. Gas lamps along the promenade wait to be lit, the church blazes gold as if the walls themselves were the source of light, glowing against the darkening sky. Prussian blue, sap green, renaissance gold. That morning he'd been feeling trapped, worried, ill, haggard – the exciting things seemed to be happening elsewhere – but now he knew that tomorrow, or next week, or next year, what he wanted would come to him and this *ganse megillah* – life, art, everything – would end in a wonderful climax, an infinite embrace, and really, all he could do was open his face up into a smile.

And the fairies at the next table smiled back.

■ Mauro invites me to his gig at Marypili, a lesbian bar on Carrer de Joan Tarrida. I sit close to the small stage and watch him play and sing – swinging his locks, his headscarf around his neck, the music a mixture of head-banging and Springsteen and it's sad and young and full of teen spirit – and every now and then he catches my eye and grins, the way men on stage tend to smile at the women who love them.

We get drunk and head to his place – his flatmates are asleep – and what lands up happening is that after he dozes off with a joint in his hand, I stroke his stomach, follow the treasure trail down, and when he's hard, I put him in my mouth and suck until he comes. Mauro sighs, and in a short while is breathing slowly, snoring lightly beneath a row of scarves on the wall, a poster of Stand Still, the grunge band from Haifa: a headless man in a suit emerging from the sea. I watch his exposed body, almost naked, his stomach, his thick dark pubic hair, his cock soft and plump and shining with spit.

I take the circuitous route back to the hotel to increase my chances of picking someone up, which I do, a waiter who lives with his boyfriend and is out walking his dog. We jerk each other off in an alleyway, our cum dotting the cobblestones.

■ The anchorwoman says a humanitarian corridor is opening up for a few hours to let supplies in to Gaza, but then she stops and turns to the reporter next to her. He's on the phone, there seems to be a crisis, the call's from Dr Abu Elaish, a physician in Gaza who, she reminds us, has been a regular on the news since the bombing began. We can hear the doctor's voice through the phone's speaker. "I can let you hear what he's saying," the reporter says. "We can just listen... I'm a bit overwhelmed at the moment." And while the doctor is shouting over the phone in Hebrew, the reporter explains that Dr Abu Elaish has worked at Tel Hashomer Hospital near Tel Aviv and that throughout the war has feared for the safety of his family.

"Who's been hurt, Abu Elaish?" the reporter says.

"My daughters," the doctor howls. "*Habanot sheli.*"

"Tell me where you are, Abu Elaish," he says to the doctor. "Maybe they can get an ambulance to you.

But the doctor is howling *ya rab*, *ya rabi*, calling

to God, and the reporter says he cannot cut off the conversation, so he keeps talking, saying to the doctor that maybe someone in the army can hear us – you said you lived near a crossroads? And the doctor says the name of the crossroads, but I don't catch it, everything suffocating under the words *ya rab, ya rabi*.

The reporter leaves the studio, a camera following him, as he tries to deal with the crisis, to contact people he knows. The anchorwoman says we'll go over to our reporter in Ashkelon who is standing alone in the town square and I recognise the clock tower, the café next to it.

Enough.

Sadness ripping at the heart – yes, there is such a thing – and I'm crying, a wet sob, trying to catch my breath. In my head, the sound of the doctor screaming over and over – my god, my lord, *hargu et habanot sheli. Ya rab, ya rabi*, and I am crying for the doctor and his children, and for the news reporter, and for the loss, for the people, and the absurdity of a Palestinian father whose daughters have been killed by Israeli pilots uttering those words in Hebrew: *hargu et habanot sheli…* the first utterance of his grief, this horror that will be his skin, uttering these words in the language of the people who have murdered his daughters. The language, too, of those who can help him as he stands amid the ruins, howling in the fire, in the centre of that glaring blaze of grief.

III

■ In the morning the sun comes up over the water. I don't have to get up for its rays to warm my face. I lie and listen to the sea, to the metronomic lapping of waves gently falling, punctuated by the whoosh of a passing car. The view from my bed is the balcony's railings, their cobalt green, palm trees, the sky, the calm water that the sun turns silver, so bright that it dazzles.

I want only honesty, true things, essence. Let's not even think what London's grey mornings have been doing to me, what the psyche is having to go through after thirty years of Mediterranean heat and blue skies, then this transition into greyness. Here in Spain the winter sunlight is the light of home, the beach, the sea, people's faces... and the war in the background, the news of more and more dead – the father repeating over and over they've killed my daughters – and now, here, in some kind of liminal space, a purgatory of sorts, neither condemned nor free. Persecuted and unbound. Bed is the only haven, everything that has happened, what I heard last night, ringing in my head, the way a few years ago they'd shown (on a loop) footage of the planes flying into the Twin Towers, all of that, as if I'm still in the dream-realm, as if reality is elsewhere, far from the vantage point of my bed.

Someone cycles along the promenade to work, a

man stands at the water's edge while his dog barks at the waves, and across the way, a woman in marigold gloves cleans the roof garden. The noise of construction work starts up nearby. *You will love him with all your heart and all your soul and all your might and you will teach these words* – to whom? to whom? I have no children. To the dead, the dead. To the dead – *when you lie down and when you rise up, when you walk along the way, you will bind them to your hands and to your forehead. You will bind them to your doors and gates for as long as there is an earth, for as long as there is a heaven.*

■ After lunch and a walk through the old town, after a visit to Can Ferrat (Rusiñol's house on the sea), I sit in Café Roy on Carrer de les Parellades, and write about Gertler and Marjorie in Sitges, about Gertler's desire to sunbathe on a particular rock all week, the rock just under Rusiñol's house, the home he built in 1895 out of two fishermen's huts and called it The Forger's Den. But really, Gertler is here to see Picasso. He'd heard the artist was staying at Rusiñol's. He would go over and make sure Mister Pablo Picasso understood that not all English art was pretty and sentimental. He was ready to tell Señor Picasso that a) he did not like his ballet and b) he did not like his scenery. Very nice, very fine, but not for me. Though by the time he got to Rusiñol's, Picasso had upped and taken the train back to Barcelona. And there was Rusiñol, combing his beard with his fingers, rising from his day-bed to greet the English guest.

I make notes about the blue of the walls in his house, a blue like no other Gertler had seen, the way the brass trays stood out against it, indanthrene blue, indigo. That blue, a language so foreign it would need immersion to learn it, an immersion akin to madness, disappearing into something bigger – you'd need to abandon England for that – so it shouldn't have come as a surprise that as soon as he got back to the kind of light that neither demanded nor facilitated intensity, he forgot about...

■ The nurse with the bell calls the patients to dinner. More often than not it's a gentle sound, at other times it's the din of a crazed flamenco dancer, and still at others, like now, as they sit on the verandah, Ottoline and Gertler, him with his eyes closed, the winter sun on his face, it sounds, Ottoline says, like in a previous life the nurse had been a cow in an Alpine meadow.

"I've become a lazy dog," Gertler says, in his almost crystal state of hunger, head light from fresh air and coughing blood, nothing left to weigh him down, nothing to keep him on the ground. His vision blurring and when, earlier that morning, he'd stood by the window to paint, the trees became cones of green, one branch indistinguishable from the next, an impression, as if the landscape was not earth and rock, but an oil painting in itself.

"You keep disappearing," Ottoline says.

"Oh, Ottoline," Gertler says. "I'm so bored."

"Don't concentrate so much," she says.

He pulls the blanket up to his neck, gathers it into a ball, hugs it to his chest. He'll write to Carrington after dinner. If it wasn't for her he'd have gone mad in here. There is no one else in the world – no one, anywhere – with whom he can be honest. Even with Ottoline he has to behave, hold back, be careful not to disrupt.

She'd driven up from Garsington with snapshots of them playing croquet on the lawn. Virginia in a lace shawl in a deck-chair, hair tied back, a hat with a feather, next to Lytton and Maynard, all very sombre. From what Gertler remembers, by the time he'd climbed back up to the house from the pond, where he and Gide and Gide's "nephew" had been watching John Murray's brother, Arthur, floating naked in a boat – too beautiful for words – Virginia and the men had their hats off and were sharing a joke with Ottoline behind the camera. The perfect atmosphere for a new painting, he thought, and dashed upstairs for his easel and paints.

"My loyal paint box," he says. "My easel, my brushes, the very same with which I struggle in London."

"But you painted this morning," she says.

"For the first time in months."

In his vest and underwear, slowly, his depression like

mud, colours oozing out like pigment from his own flesh. Sometimes – he hasn't forgotten this – it is pure joy.

"You'll be home by the summer," Ottoline says.

"You know what it's like?" he says. "It's like there's this person you love very much, but you only see them every now and again and then only among other people, always in a bustle... and suddenly... one day... you and your beloved are alone in a room, just the two of you, and you're not quite sure what to say."

That day at Garsington, walking with his easel and paints back to the pond where the sun sliced through the trees and etched itself onto Arthur Murray's alabaster skin.

"*Un specimen tres bon, non?*" Gide said.

They sat on deck chairs, Gide smoking, bald, eyes squinting – all the better to see you with – and Forster with his head buried (*plus ça change*) in a newspaper, all three obscured by the tall hedge around the pond, hidden from the house, all the better to watch the goings on of a young boy of twenty with taut flesh and a full head of hair, bobbing back and forth on a boat, fingers trailing in the water.

"He'll die one day," Gide had added.

Ottoline touched his cheek.

"I'll have to go soon," she said.

And before you know it, heavy drops of rain are plopping against the window.

"I'm sorry to be so tiresome," Gertler said.

"There's a photograph missing," she said, pointing to the gap on the page.

"What does the caption say?"

They bow their heads, each waiting for the other to read aloud, but they remain silent. Three months since Katherine's death. Had she been there that day, that perfect day at Garsington, when he'd set up his easel to face the house and begin his work on *The Pond at Garsington*?

■ My last night in Sitges and I'm eating dinner alone: a salad of raw cod with anchovies and tuna on a mound of lettuce, so intense I keep eating from the bowl of olives to modify the shock. It's exciting and overwhelming to eat raw flesh, the impact unmitigated by talk or sound. So I'm scribbling this to you, Gabriel, using these tangled threads of cursive, each word a lost beetle marking the page, a roller-coaster ride in miniature. Interrupted by the arrival of a seafood risotto, creamy and pink, a single chive laid diagonally across the rice. I eat slowly, my body still reeling from the jolt of raw cod, the delicacy of the cooked dish now inspiring restraint and reverence. For dessert: crema catalana with a chocolate cigarillo across the top, echoing the risotto's chive. Are we being given a metaphor, a symbol for the thin line, a fissure to ingest, the crack that lets in the light, the broken who illumine the world.

"I fucking love these," the woman behind me says.

She's in her mid-forties, South African. The man with her is older, his voice gravelly, a smoker's voice, words that tumble into each other, barely distinguishable. She says the word "relationship" so many times I stop hearing anything else and listen only to the bass line that is "relationship... relationship..." quieter and quieter each time until she goes silent – *falls* silent – and he begins to speak. He's her therapist, some strange guru-therapist who has his sessions over dinner, who has cultivated a deep and soothing tone no matter what he's talking about. She and her husband are about to get divorced.

"And I'm supposed to speak rationally about it?" she says, biting loudly into another something. "I can't. It's driving me mad."

"Your anger is coming between you and your relationship," the therapist says. "That's number one. There's too much in your life and too much in his life. You have an obligation to the children."

His sentences get swallowed by their loud crunching, and by his voice that is a kind of growl, as if his words were phlegm to hawk up: "Sometimes people have a hard time saying what they feel. For a long time I couldn't express my true feelings. But I could write them down," he says. "I learnt to express them through writing."

And then as if to answer the noisy food question,

the waiter brings me a saucer of rolled-up biscuits, the kind you buy in tins, stacked close together to prevent breakage, and a flagon of wine, a rosé, almost transparent, the decanter nestled in a wicker cradle. I'm suddenly aware of the tablecloth, the colour of oxidised copper, as if this has all been preparation for a still life. Am I supposed to pour the wine into a glass (but where is the glass?) or onto the biscuits? Sometimes a request for knowledge is akin to a confession. I eat the gaufrettes, four exclamation marks, a satisfying and unequivocal end to dinner before heading back to my room to call Gabriel.

■ "How convenient," he says, "to stumble upon a painter in the middle of your project."

"You don't think people will believe it?"

"I'm not sure it works in the context of your narrative," he says. "They might wonder why this big love of yours isn't with you in Sitges."

"I told you why."

"I still don't buy it," he says. "Anyway, are you having fun?"

"Not at the moment," I say. "Did I tell you what happened on the beach?"

"Is this going to be another sex story? I think I'm ready for the monogamy conversation."

A crowd had gathered on the beach opposite the

hotel, about thirty people around a man in a black Speedo on his back in the sand so thin that the bones in his shoulders and hips looked as if they could slice through his skin. Another man, a man who must have been his friend, told another man that the man in the sand had come here to die. He used the phrase "give up the ghost." He said this is where he'd been infected, in the caverns of the sauna on Carrer de Sant Bonaventura, by some German who'd come inside him. The dead man was so high on something, so full of love, that he wanted the German to infect him.

"He'd lived a good life," said the man, muscular like a boxer with flecks of white in his chest-hair. His deep tan made him look rugged, weathered, and he spoke like he'd rehearsed this story, maybe even with the dead man himself, sharing it now with us, as if this were a wake and we the mourners reluctant to let the body go, delaying the moment we'd have to give the nod to the one in charge of closing the casket.

"How will you get him back to London?" someone asked.

He'd arranged to be cremated, have his ashes scattered into the sea from the rock where he and the German had sat at five in the morning after their first night together and watched the sun come up.

"You're lying," Gabriel says.

"Not much," I say.

"You're a mendicant."

"Is that a compliment?"

"You make people say and behave the way you want them to."

"It's my job," I say.

"But what'll happen when you write about me?" he says. "You'll have me saying and doing things according to your likes and dislikes."

"What do you want me to say about that?"

"You make it sound naïve," he says. "It's libelous. No wonder you have so many ex-friends and always talk about being isolated."

"But that's Gertler," I say. "Not me."

Telephones can bring us together and turn us into savages, bring out the blood-lust in us, make it easier to cause harm.

"Tell me about your day," I say.

"Not now," he says.

■ Later that night, Mauro comes up to my room so he can play Radiohead and Pearl Jam for me on his iPod dock. It's three in the morning, we're stoned and naked, and I can see he's regretting this. He lies on the bed and I kneel beside him, my head level with his body. He is silent and I am silent, there is nothing to say. I can tell from his eyes, from the way his mouth is shut, that he is beyond caring. The streetlamps cast a dull yellow light onto everything: his skin, the sheets, the wallpaper, all the same colour – doughy.

"It's not going to work," he says.

"What's wrong with the way it is?"

"It's not what I want," he says, and turns onto his side to look at me, his locks spreading across the pillow like a child's drawing of the sun and its rays.

"Why did you come up?"

"I like being with you," he says.

"Then why can't we keep doing this?"

I gather his hair into a sheaf so that his face and neck are exposed.

"You want more than I can give," he says.

"You have to fuck someone," I say. "Why not let it be me?"

"I don't," he says, and turns to face the ceiling. "Can we stop this, please."

"Can I lie next to you?"

He says nothing, but moves over to make room. I tell him how Gertler killed himself in his late forties, around the time of his son's seventh birthday. I tell him that he used to come to Sitges with his wife and other writers and painters, that he'd tried to meet Picasso, but Picasso had left for Barcelona. Eventually we fall asleep, Mauro facing one way, me the other, the edges of our buttocks touching.

In the morning – just three hours sleep – Mauro

goes downstairs for breakfast duty and I sit on the edge of the bed watching the palm trees and the sea. In the terra cotta pots on the edge of the balcony, the daisies are bright yellow. The woman with the marigold gloves is still cleaning the adjacent roof garden. These days in Sitges have been full of the warmth of the winter-sun and the sound of waves. I've opened the glass doors in the morning, stayed under the duvet and slept my post-breakfast nap with the sun on my face, then reawakened to stare at the sea until the sun made its way up and over the upstair's balcony and put me back in the shade. Soon I'll be home again. Gabriel will be there to meet me. Mauro will continue to oversee breakfast, play grunge to the lesbians. From what I can hear, it sounds like someone in the room next door is making early-morning love.

■ A white tablecloth, a clay decanter, two glasses, a loaf of bread, strawberries on a white saucer. He can smell the orange juice, the strawberries. The bread is clay. (*He'll never love you. He cannot love a woman. He's a half-dead thing.*) Soon he will paint. Drink the juice. Eat the bread, nibble the strawberries. *Don't swallow them whole.* There is time. In the quiet of his studio, seeds crack in the cavern of his mouth, lips on fruit, kissing, a child practising for the arrival of the prince.

Don't get me wrong, she writes, *I'm not going to say*

that's why I'll take sugar in my coffee now, though taking sugar does make one appreciate the poets more. I only like sugar in my coffee sometimes, not every week, not every day. I think you like it so much you'd gladly take it so often that in time you'll taste nothing. You can have three lumps a month. Now you've had more than three, so no more till January.

But joking aside.

I'm sorry for being so tiresome, you cannot imagine the difficulties inside me. I envy the ones who love simply, less selfishly than you and I. My new painting excites me. It is all I want to do all day. I shall go for a long walk later over the Downs. But it's almost too cold outside for me to be really happy.

Not long after, a letter to thank him for his patience, to say he cannot know how she hates herself sometimes. *Often.* What upset her most was his dishonesty, saying he didn't know if it had gone right up. *You were selfish and lazy and you took a risk.* More than anything, she wants to live, and thoughts of the consequences fill her with horror. None of this must ever be talked about, and, if possible, if he would please (*yes, she knows it's impossible*) refrain from sharing this with the grand gossips of Garsington.

I do so love the big picture you're working on — it will be tremendous when it's completed! The tulips are the greatest still life he's ever done. *I'm so proud of you,* she writes, and signs her letter: *Your Periwinkle Crinkle Crinkle*.

Dear Carrington. If you are reading this I am dead. I have carried out what I knew I would. Almost forty and I am gone. Marjorie will tell you how they found my body in the sea. I'm sorry I never came to visit you in the months before this and that this death has drawn you back to me. I wanted it to be love, but you have ground the strength of my love to dust. This is my way of exploding in your path – to have you walking along and bang, to shock you into regret, pity, longing.

Their last meeting at the Tour Eiffel Café in London, the final goodbye, a harsh and honest ending where she'd made it clear she would live with Strachey, regardless of the question of the physical.

"I never want to see you again," he said. "I will leave after breakfast."

"I don't blame you," she said.

"Don't you see how young and beautiful you are? I cannot see you again, not unless you change and love me. Better to stop now than become enemies."

They drank their orange juice, ate their toast, and got up to leave. While he was paying, he noticed Carrington watching him. She'd want them to walk together towards Tottenham Court Road.

"Don't think I'm angry with you," he said. "I'm not

angry," he said. "Farewell."

Goodbye.

He walks down Charlotte Street, she back up to the flat on Gower Street where the housekeeper will open the door, and Lytton will be there in the study and nobody will know how it had all ended with Mark.

London I

❧

■ Standing at the lights on Piccadilly on my way to meet Gabriel at the William Nicholson exhibition. Fortnum and Mason's behind me, doors opening, closing, people striding in and out on their way to somewhere, another stop on this endless safari for the perfect bargain. Winter in London, post-Christmas, the Time of the Sales, a kind of rapaciousness, different to the urgency of Christmas shopping. Having spent December pleasing others, now there is license for self-indulgence.

The lights change and I cross the road, my spirits lifting as I walk through the arches of the Royal Academy towards a beautiful man sitting on the steps of a statue, sketching.

"It's so nice outside," Gabriel says, from the top step, a foot taller than me. I move closer and rest my head on his chest. "Let's walk to the river," he says.

We head towards Haymarket, stopping off at Paxton and Whitfield on Jermyn Street for some gjetost, a sweet

Norwegian cheese that we eat like fudge, breaking off small pieces. Ahead of us, a father and son are playing a game of tag, until the father lifts his son up, hugs him, then swings him from his feet so he's hanging upside down.

"Pure wombat," Gabriel says.

And it's like Barcelona again, the closeness between us. I'm at my best when I have a hand in mine. As long as you keep holding my hand, I will never leave. It's that simple, that unevolved. I don't care what people say. And they don't say anything, but they look. People look at men holding hands.

"What if we all held hands?" I say. "If we all went around holding hands. Tim and Anup, Raffaele and Simon, Michael and Andy, RJ and Mike, Andrew and Nadav, Emmanuel and David, everyone, all of us, and me with my hand in yours."

"There's the issue of your book," Gabriel says. "People will believe all these things about you."

"And about you, too."

"They'll think you're leaving nothing unexposed."

"I'm trying not to," I say.

"Then how about a happy ending for this one?"

A man selling poetry on Hungerford Bridge lays his pamphlets out on a blanket, like the Albanians – Bulgarians? Uzbeks? – who sell key rings of miniature London buses and tiny Big Bens. Tourists stand against the railings taking pictures with the London Eye in the background.

"I'm not sure I can do happy endings," I say. "Not the kind you're talking about. But a good hand-job!" I say. "Would that be an ending you'd like?"

"Definitely," he says.

With soup and sandwiches, we head for the sofas in the lobby of the Royal Festival Hall. Children dart amongst the columns. Everything is white: the sofas, the tables, these columns erected to emit sounds of nature from embedded speakers: birdsong, a fox's call, water trickling over rocks. We sit on a sofa and eat our lunch, then Gabriel naps while I write, his head against my stomach, warm and soothing, his fingers twitching in his lap – a dream? a longing to paint? – to the recorded sounds of finches and brooks and crickets, and it's early enough in the day for us to feel, this chance gathering of people in this lobby transformed into a sunken garden, to imagine that this is ours, that there is room enough for all of us to be what we want to be, taking pleasure in the intimacy of unplanned association while out there people shop or go to church or head off to war.

■ A sudden ceasefire, a pause in the ruin of Rafah and the tunnels, the bombing of food supplies, the telling of soldiers to do whatever it takes – all silenced. Children transform the rubble of their homes into playgrounds, something to clamber up and be king of the castle, destruction to carry through into the next generation. A few have seen their uncles make bombs out of medicine bottles, their brothers booby-trap the mosques, send rockets into Ashkelon – but didn't you tell us, *tata*, that that's where you're from? If one didn't have to go to work or to the gym, to have dinner with a lover, one could get caught up in all this drama. Now the forgetting can begin, a way of preparing for the inevitable horrors to come. That's how we function, those of us who have grown up in the war zones of the world.

■ I'm the one who says no to everything. I am the one who the one who I am the one who. I am the one who says maybe. Especially maybe. I am the beginning, the sperm, the ashes. I am the one who says perhaps. Perhaps maybe. The one who says maybe yes and maybe... maybe we should be doing something else instead of plopping into conformity like frogs. I am the toad and the prince, the gargoyle and the queen. The water and the fire. The one who drowns his lovers in messy pleadings.

I am bigger than I think, fatter, not as generous nor as sweet. You should see some of the things I've done. I've done things that would shock most mothers, things that shock even me when I'm in a more traditional mood. Shocked by things I have seen, though when I tell Gabriel about this while we sit in the sunken foyer-garden of the

Royal Festival Hall, tell him between sips of camomile tea… but isn't that normal? Isn't the anxiety and dread in my body palpable? This fury, this burning, as if I'm about to explode. Why shouldn't I be telling him this? Who else is there to tell? We've been lovers for long enough, for months, both of us refugees in this city, in exile, not as destitute as men in the belly of a truck, nor rolling in it like *fin-de-siècle* emigrés in Paris. Far from it. But refugees, nonetheless.

Okay fine, I think. I won't tell you the details.

Memory is a crowd of bodies grappling for attention, most of them naked, most of them naked.

I'm not good when it comes to the pain of getting to know someone, of being born into something new. When I start to think about it I just want to rest my head in my hands and sleep. I mean weep. Gabriel walks off – he does – and what I should have done is tell him the truth, tell him everything that happened, instead of standing there like a fish-wife.

"What did you want?" he says. "Did you expect me to come back and hold your hand?"

"You could have waited," I say.

We walk in silence, me eating the rest of a Kit-Kat.

"Do you want some?"

"I've had enough junk food for a week," he says.

"What's enough?" I say.

"A Mars bar," he says. "And jelly babies."

"And?"

"Can we talk about last night," he says.

"We should head back," I say. "They close at six."

And so we do, back to the Nicholson exhibition at the Royal Academy. Standing before paintings, separating colours, trying to name the different paints, the way each touch of paint is an echo of the thing. Nicholson makes his silver in "Silver" out of white and black and lime and sap green, titanium white, Payne's grey, ochre. All the time Gabriel and I close together, shoulders touching, fingers brushing against each other. Rejoicing in this naming of colours. The chrome yellow of "The Gold Jug": raw umber, green, charcoal, vermilion, yellow.

A still life is a portrait of absence.

The slowing down of noticing.

But we have to talk, I think. There are things you need to know.

■ What they landed up doing, the two of them, their last time together at Garsington, after the quarrel – what they landed up doing was to sit in silence on the sofa with their books in their laps. Carrington absorbed in Lytton's new book, Gertler feeling her being pulled away, although no one was doing the pulling. The man she loved did nothing but be his regular undemanding pansy of a self. She and Gertler on the sofa seemingly composed. That's what Ottoline must have seen when she paused at the door, adolescents who'd been spinning into a frenzy, raging at each other with unfulfilled lust, now calm.

"Chekhov," Gertler says, tapping his finger on the page. "This man's a genius."

Ottoline had talked to Carrington last night, taken her for walks in the garden, tried to convince her that he, Gertler, was her one true love.

"Mark," Carrington says.

Moving in closer, the sleeve of her dress touches his shirt. Second skin but not flesh. She doesn't want to go over the same ground. I can't bear to make you sad, to see you like this, on your knees begging for sugar. How can you want a body that cannot give solace to anyone. Yet he knows: the way he pursues her, like a dog, relentlessly and without humour, reassures her.

"What did Ottoline say?"

"Stop," she says. "I hate this assault on all fronts."

They stare ahead. Nothing in their books can distract them from the agony ripping them apart. Nothing can rescue them. One pulls and one pulls away. Gertler turns his book over and rests it, words down, on his lap.

"They care about me," he says.

"*I* care about you," she says.

"Do you?"

"I didn't come all this way for this," she says.

"Then why did you come?"

"For you," Carrington says.

Ottoline walks in and makes herself comfortable by the window. She turns the pages of her magazine, looks out at Julian on the verandah reading a travel guide to Andalucía. Gertler can feel it happening, building up to some brutal ending, their bodies stranded on a sofa, afloat, out at sea – no, on a bed, on a bed – her resistance intensifying his hunger, every *no* a beckoning, every inch of exposed flesh – a wrist, a neck, an ankle – mocking him, a child calling out in a game of tag: *You can't catch me.*

Later that evening, he calls his brother in London and implores him to come and get him. Rushes through goodbyes to Ottoline, to Turner, whoever's there, fighting the sadness that threatens to kill him, everything growing dark – to think that just a few hours ago he'd been sitting by the pond watching

butterflies

a baby girl.

remnants of a blue sky. And in his room upstairs, packed and ready to leave: white tulips, purple tulips in a vase by the window. Outside, treetops and the corner of the barn, the scent of pine. He'd never learnt the names of trees (*ah, oui*, Gide had said, trying to teach him in French, to say *pin, chêne, cèdre – but the hunger to know so much more noble than the knowing itself*). He drew them in shapes, wholes, no detail of bark and branch and leaf. Impressions fed by East End animism and his time at Clayton and Bell, preparing the stained glass windows for the Catholic Chapel at Westminster. Why can't this, now, be all there is: roses clinging to the wall outside his window, pink, yellow, this vase of tulips. To capture this, not the patchwork of crowded buildings, narrow streets, the family dragged back to Europe then back to London, market stalls, traders on Elder Street, hooves on cobblestones like the popping a child makes, finger to the inside of the mouth, then out. He stands there, *pop*, *pop*, silencing the chatter, laughter, drowning out thoughts of what is now clear: She will never be his. All is grey, and what the evening had promised, whatever it was going to be, was now murky and bleak and all he wants is home.

Brighton

■ The day Gala came to visit Dali he was in his studio boiling up a glue of fish bones and goat shit to rub into his chest and arms, but when he saw her through the window, those piercing eyes, the high forehead, the condescending smile, the way she marched towards the house, he washed it all off, put on a pearl necklace, stuck a geranium behind his ear, and in a fit of giggles, scurried out to welcome her.

"*Bienvenida!*" he declared.

In the three months before sex, Dali jerked off and painted *The Great Masturbator* – Gala emerging from his head, his limp penis level with her nose. Where his mouth should have been – a locust, symbol of the starved souls of men. She was the man-eating praying mantis. It's with your blood I created this, then signed the painting with her name and his.

"She inspired and mothered, nursed, marketed, and tortured him for fifty year. They transformed each other into the gods of their own mythology."

"I'm not sure what you're trying to tell me," Gabriel says. "Are you pulling away or checking if I love you as much as that?"

"It's not that," I say. "It's just that I feel the honeymoon stage is over."

He's trying, with the tip of his finger, to remove a speck of something from his eye. He closes both eyes and leans back on the pillow, his mouth making the shape of a smile. He looks up at me with the other eye.

"I'm having fun," he says, struggling with dust or an eyelash, talking casually as if to say he's not getting drawn into this conversation.

"It's *my* stuff," I say.

"I don't expect a honeymoon at all times," he says. "There are days I don't want to see you either, when I want to paint and there's no time. No one could survive on a constant state of overwhelming love."

"I know," I say. "You're right."

"In what way was last Friday," he says, "the day after you got back from Sitges, when we went for breakfast in the park and then to a movie, then to Kudos for a drink – how was that different to your so-called Honeymoon Stage?"

"We're so cautious with each other," I say. "We never let go. Maybe it's just me. I get into these moods, like I'm possessed, and then we're both miserable."

"Maybe it *is* just you," he says. "You confuse me with your lack of clarity."

"Stop," I say. "Let me."

He has pulled his top eyelid over the bottom.

"Hold still," I say, and put the tip of my finger against his retina.

"Voila," I say, the grit sticking to my skin.

"Thank you," he says.

"You're welcome."

"So," he says, pulling himself up to a sitting position and leaning against the wall. "Am I Gala?"

"No," I say. "*I'm* the muse."

"Not a very consistent muse," he says. "You should be helping me access the broad and sweeping emotions of love and betrayal, helpless adoration."

He pulls the duvet up to cover his legs, tucks it in around his middle, like someone waiting for a tray to be set before them.

"If you were a proper muse," he says, "the answers to great ontological puzzles would be flashing before my eyes. Even at this very minute, as we speak, even before we start to fuck."

"Oh, gosh," I say.

"Yes, gosh," he says. "I'm not sure you're equipped to be a muse. You can't even commit to this weekend in Brighton."

"Watch me," I say.

■ The basement flat by the sea has patches of mildew on the walls, the smell of damp hits you when you walk in – it sticks to everything: the walls, the furniture, your skin. The decor is pure IKEA: rugs, bed linen, the chest of drawers, the coffee table.

"I feel so lucky," I say.

"I, on the other hand, feel like we should be staying at the Metropole."

"The Metropole?" I say, putting my arm around his waist and kissing him.

"Like the Gertlers," he says.

"You remembered."

"I *do* listen," Gabriel says.

From the top of the steps leading from the flat to the pavement, just the sky behind him, flanked by a low wall, he stands there as if to block my way, as if it'll cost me to cross the bridge.

"Name your price," I say.

He leans forward, a brief kiss, three seconds, maybe four, but it's the kind of kiss that is knowing, that knows the mouth of the other, the way the lips fit together, soft, the tips of our tongues touching, without entering each other's mouths, and because we're by the seaside, because we're together, because a gentle kiss between men in public – yes, and in private! – is still a political act, even if this is Brighton, even if we're outside the Amsterdam Hotel, and because it's warm and the sun is shining and the sky is blue and Gabriel is taller than me at this moment – I can look up to him... everything... this time... this place... the mild weather... will always be remembered.

"Let's perambulate," he says.

I tell him about Gertler the chatterer, the storyteller, the impersonator, the one who dresses up, wears silly hats, strips naked, the one who irritated Virginia Woolf for talking endlessly about his favourite subject – himself! – the one who kept the party going, the one they tried to seduce, the funny one – *oh, the Jews! What a laugh!* – but I fear that the tone, all that's coming out of me, the subtext that is my text, everything I do when I'm with someone, this tormented narrative I carry with me, is a story at odds with my potential.

"Because deep down," I say to Gabriel. "I'm a happy person."

"Hilarious," he says.

"Fuck off."

"But that's exactly why I like you," he says.

"Why?"

"Because you're happy," he says. "An outright happy individual with a natural *joie de vivre*."

"I could be Gertler," I say. "The life and soul. He tried to be a writer, you know. When his paintings wouldn't sell, and he couldn't bring himself to keep going, he began a misery memoir, the story of his life. He figured the people he knew in publishing would help him sell the book. He wrote about the poverty he grew up in, his depression, the messed-up relationship with his father, the way his mother moaned about her useless husband. It didn't take him long to realise that there's no redemption in writing, and if there is, it would take more time to materialise than he had at his disposal, much longer than a painting. It was the *ganse megillah* or nothing, all or nothing at all."

"I could never write," Gabriel says.

"Maybe trying to write, and failing... maybe that's what sent him back to painting.

"Or suicide," he says.

The waves make that particular sound you get on a pebble beach, not the single crashing sound of a wave on a sandy shore. Here each stone, each pebble, each empty shell makes itself known, its jingle, swish and echo. A man with flippers stands at the water's edge. The incline from shore to sea is abrupt, and he steps cautiously into the water – the sun may be warm, but it's mid-winter. He sets off from the shore, his cap, his black swimming trunks, the rubber of his flippers marked against his skin tones, burnt sienna, yellow ochre, cadmium orange.

"Why couldn't you write?" I say.

"Why can't you paint?"

"Is it that simple?" I say. "Either you can or can't?"

"Or you won't and don't."

"I *do* want to paint," I say.

"I love these moments," he says. "I love you."

"Don't spoil it."

"But I *do* love these moments," he says. "You're so beautiful when you're like this."

"I told you," I say. "I'm a happy person."

"How about fish and chips?" he says. "On me."

There's something about Brighton, about being by the sea, this vast expanse of water, walking along the promenade with the horizon to our right. Something precise, reminiscent, as if this is what the world was like to begin with, this is what childhood was like: to your left – the known (buildings, windows, people) and to your right – a vast openness, possibility. The concrete and hypothetical, and us walking between them. Traffic flows, the sun sets, a man swims parallel to the shoreline, and all that lies ahead is the simple question: haddock or cod?

■ The Gertler *mishpucheh* arrived in Brighton like a caravan of refugees emptied out onto Platform 6. What they liked about Brighton was the food. There was a *yid* with a fish shop in Kemp Town who made a whole vat of pickled herring to feed those who schlepped to the coast for a weekend paddle. No one could swim, Gertler included, but they liked the horizon, walking on the promenade, sitting in a café, watching the waves plop onto the pebbled shore.

The Metropole – his brothers were paying – was full of Jews and Americans. His older brothers had a couple of girls with them, pretty in evening dresses, bare arms. Gertler sat and drank and watched the Jews eat. In a strange way it reminded him of Paris. The lights, the strolling, the cafés with big windows, a sense that time could wind down, move slower, away from the constant onslaught of London. There were days in London, misty and stuffy, when he felt as if his head had been shoved into an oven. The Lawrences had been visiting… his time with them – awkward. He didn't want to be around all that coughing and wheezing, the spitting of blood, the talk of Hardy's slow decline. Old age depressed him. Is that all there was to look forward to after thirty? Was that it?

"*Ikh hob lib* Brighton," he says to his mother. "I'll *shraybn a bukh* about it one day."

They are on a bench in the conservatory looking out to sea.

"Make a painting," she says.

"That, too," he says.

Beyond the lights on the promenade the horizon has disappeared. Darkness is an expanse. He likes an entire something spread out before him, a landscape to be captured, the lawns at Garsington, the sea. The plan was to eventually tackle the whole landscape question one day, the incongruity of a Jew in nature. The stifling bucolic imperative of the English countryside reminded him of his own disease. He could feel his mother breathing next to him, in and out, as if exhaling the reality of the East End, painting over it with every intake of salty sea air. What could she be thinking, so far from everything she has known, all the water she'll never see again, lakes dipped in, seas crossed.

She pats his knee, then rests her hand warm against his.

"*Mamele,*" he says. "*Tants mit mir.*"

■ In the morning, Gabriel does his push-ups and sit-ups, then chin-ups on a bar attached to the door jamb. Naked and hanging, skin pulled taut across torso, nipples small and pink, urchin shells on sand, soft hair in his armpits, a belly-button disappearing. From the vantage point of our bed, I count the times he brings his chin to the bar: thirteen, fourteen, fifteen... his body an exclamation mark, his biceps long. Nineteen. Twenty.

"I've been thinking about going off the dole," he says, shaking his arms, pacing the room.

My mind is still on his body, the way it feels against mine, especially when we stand side by side in a bar, at a pedestrian crossing waiting for the lights to change, by the kitchen window looking out over North London, the way we slot into each other, what it feels like when I put my arm around his waist and draw him to me, press him against my side like he was part of me.

"Come back to bed."

"I'm sick of this poverty," he says.

"You'd get distracted by work," I say.

"I hate this constant lack of funds," he says.

"Use the dole to paint," I say. "It's the state's way of paying you to work."

"An artist on £60 a week!"

"Come here," I say.

"Don't patronise me."

"Come,"

"We've been stuck in this basement for weeks!"

"We arrived yesterday."

"I'm cold," he says. "Brighton's cold and damp."

"There's the sauna. We could go to the sauna."

Yesterday we had cod and chips, tomorrow we'll be in London, but today we're at the bakery on St James's Street in Brighton. Croissants and pain aux raisins while we walk like tourists around Kemp Town... walking and eating and drinking, and it's leisurely, evoking the word "amble": moving without expectation, coffee and pastries in hand, a tall slender man at my side, young and beautiful, the taste of his sweat from morning exercises still on my lips. I am the envy of the street, I've made it and I am – say it – the bomb! Hit the jackpot. Gold struck. Gabriel responds to it, too – this swagger of mine – coffee in one hand and my elbow in the other and I feel depended upon, solid, I feel – oh, fuck it – like a man.

It's been confirmed: phosphorous bombs were used, food and fuel supplies were shelled, innocent people were shot... and we pause at the corner of St James Street and Devonshire Place, breathing in the salt air, the sea in front of us.

A tree shows its buds, tiny green leaves opening up. I reach into the branches and stroke a white blossom, nature's silent gesture of spring.

Even this early in the day, even with so few people here, the sauna is an oasis of warmth, a retreat. Stripped down to nothing, towels around our waists, we have come to hunt. The other two men in the locker room are the kind with slick hairstyles and waxed chests and they stare at Gabriel.

"You ready?" I say.

"A quick swim first," he says, stepping closer, his smile going from suggestive to open to questioning. "My man," he says. "You are so beautiful."

"Stop it," I say.

"You are. And when you're ready," he says. "I want to know everything."

If we hadn't been in the locker room, if we hadn't been whispering into each other's mouths, about to enter the caverns to have sex with strangers, I would have relinquished my hold on a story of a young man whose death I carry with me like a shell.

"Let's hunt," he says.

Out of the locker room and into the showers!

A man in the middle of the swimming pool holds onto the ankles of another man, turning him slowly in a circle, the floating man's body stiff, eyes closed, arms at his side. Skinny and slight, like a shard slicing through water. The standing man keeps his eyes on the floating man, and they both turn, their pace torpid, like it could be a dream, the standing man turning on the spot, the floating man creating ripples on the water's surface.

One is the lighthouse, the other – a beacon of light.

"But I need to swim my laps," I say.

"Don't be grumpy."

"I'll wait until they're done."

In this sanctuary from society's expectations, we are part of a tradition. We come to bathe and preen, beautify ourselves for our lovers, meet friends, play games, have a snack, get a back-rub. Free from the threat of war. We will not be attacked or ridiculed. Rejection is gentle, the worst that can happen is he'll walk away or tap your hand. No fear of physical violence, never the question: will he beat me up? Once, in Prague, a young man slapped my hand. But that was all, his gesture revealing more about his bad manners than any inherent flaw on my part. That same day, another man told me he'd fallen in love with me. Places like these, in a strange way, are the height of civility: no violence, no threat of carnage. Beyond these white walls, beyond the faux Roman decor, the large palm trees, the mural of Caesar above the pool, we are exposed to the constancy of hate.

Whitney Houston sings anything you want done bay-hay-bee, and the men in the pool make me smile. The floating man raises his head and looks into the eyes of the standing man, and even while his ankles are still in the hands of the other man, the floating man bends his body inwards until his arms are around the standing man, like they've done this before, and the standing man lifts the floating man into the air so he's upright, his body above water – he is the lighthouse now, he is the lighthouse – and the standing man propels him into the air. The flying man arches his body and dives backwards, chest out, face to the sky, and silently re-enters the pool.

I am not the only one to witness this moment. The two well-groomed men from the locker room are at the opposite end of the pool. They walk towards me, our eyes on each other – two against one – and they keep walking, our gazes fixed, turning their heads slightly as they make their way towards the steam room.

When two animals stare at each other, one will, at some point, roll onto its back, as if to say: I'd rather be fucked than killed. We're a bit like that, we'd much rather take it up the arse than through the heart. We also, particularly those of us who come to places like these, like to look. We stare, as if only we can see the s-t-a-r in stare, then we roll over onto our backs to assume the posish.

"I'm ready," we say.

Naked and in public, unashamed amongst strangers. I'm on the terracotta ledge in the steam room with the muscled groomed men opposite me. We wait to see who'll make the first move. The men from the pool – the one who stands and the one who flies – come in and sit together on a ledge of their own. We are five. I want to record these moments before we touch, before it all begins – "it" being the kissing and sucking, the pulling and tugging, the surprises, the inevitabilities. Anticipation and doubt. In these before-moments, I want all of them. I'm like that, wanting everyone. Fated to be here, gathered for just this reason, uncluttered, brazen. There's something jubilant about it, about this electricity of potential, being both performance and audience, waiting for the show to begin, the show that is us.

The flying man makes the first move.

Skin like warm plastic, no, velvet, like paper, no, canvas, a page... in this place where we are wet with sweat and water, the skin soft and clear. His eagerness excites me, his kneeling, the way he insists on rubbing the back of his throat with my cock, so gaunt, so voluptuous in his hunger, not unlike many skinny men I've known, much more appealing than large men with appetites to match their bulk.

Then Gabriel walks in. A party guest newly arrived, unsure if he's in the right room – *am I interrupting?* – no, this is where you belong. For a moment, with my arm around his waist, I think he is Gertler, that this is what it would feel like to be so close, to hold him naked, his body pressed against mine. How do you gauge time when you let go into passion, when you stop resisting, stop observing from the outside. I can't tell how long we do this, Gabriel, Gertler, me, our tongues in each other's mouths, before a fourth man joins us, one of the men with muscles, and his oversized penis and I remember thinking how odd to see a cock like this on display, carried around so nonchalantly, now in my hand, an act of beneficence, shared with strangers.

The concealment of body parts is supposed to keep sexual curiosity alive, but here we are, men naked, and our curiosity for the soul increases, those wounded, loving, glorious bits that make us vulnerable and hungry for love. We're in love in the steam room, a camaraderie of desire, love radiating out from our core, full of glee, the four of us, like kings, everything we want we have: beauty, riches, vast territories. We toil fiercely, free of worry. I kneel on the warm terracotta floor while the other two, the standing man and the other man with muscles, from their respective ledges, sit and watch, as if we are the children and they the gods before whom we play. As if they're the ones on shore, and we, out amongst the waves – the bathers.

■ In the dream, the truck leaves the parking lot outside Kiryat Shmona, the road lined with pine trees. We're moving towards the border and I have this gut feeling this will be my last time in Lebanon, that the truck's going to be attacked, or we'll be captured, shot, and I want to tell someone they've made a mistake, that I'm not in the army anymore, that I don't have to be here, that I live in London now. Ask anyone, I say, and point to my mother and father who are on the side of the road, leaning against their VW Combi van, bright orange, waving and smiling, though we all know my father is dead – my mother shrugs: *What can you do? He just turned up!* – and my sister sits cross-legged on the roof of the van drinking hot chocolate from a flask. The woman who works as a cleaner for my mother, whose son was killed in the first days of the war, and who could never say my name and always called me *Schultz*, she's there in a floral dress and headscarf, arms folded across her chest. An old friend from high school, Shoval Kaplan, is there with his guitar slung across his shoulder like an M16 rifle, with a placard that says בוגד in red, paint dripping like blood. And I want to jump off the truck, give away my gun and my metal jacket, my helmet, my boots. But they're clapping, egging me on, all except Shoval Kaplan who keeps running after the truck with his placard screaming: *Traitor*. In the dream I tell myself: You can wake up, your army days are over, nothing can make you stay here, but I keep sitting as we near the border, cherry trees in blossom everywhere, whitewashed villas, fields of sunflowers stretching till the horizon. And then the shooting begins.

"Can you hear that?" Gabriel says.

I hear them before I see them through the basement window, cheers and clapping, the sound of an approaching carnival, hundreds of them, like a cavalry, a shoal, the street emptying for them. Naked people on bicycles. A woman with long blonde hair covering her breasts, men, so many, bums squashed against bike seats. People on the pavement watch as they pass by. It's like something out of a fairytale, *the ladies of the harem of the court of King Caractacus*. Gabriel presses against my back, and we stand there at the window like window-shoppers.

"Gertler would have loved this," I say.

He'd have been on his bike, flaunting his smooth backside, and Monty and Eddie and Brett and everyone who'd ever wanted him, all of those who enjoyed the sight of him in the nude, would be there, Ottoline, and

Katherine and André Gide and "the nephew" and Julian, jumping up and down, cheering, running alongside, egging him on. *Go Mark. Show us what you've got.* And he would have waved and lifted his big floppy hat and shaken his curls, *look, ma, no hands*, and glided along, swimming in his own pleasure.

■ The train crawls its way back to London. I've been thinking about making the trip back, going home to confront the war. Like being summoned. But they're not your people. Only my sister is there. I don't have anyone left. She was living down south in Ashkelon until a rocket from Gaza fell close to her home and she moved to Tel Aviv with her boyfriend.

"Let's go, then," says Gabriel.

"My sister says Dizengoff is full of people shopping."

Our distractions are survival techniques. The war's happening elsewhere, death happens in another country so we can get on with our lives. Defend yourself by fighting on enemy soil. As if Israel were an island. As long as the war and destruction stay away from Tel Aviv, people can pretend there's no war.

"We'll go shopping, then," he says.

The prospect of being in Tel Aviv, booking into an hotel, being a tourist during a time of war is unexpectedly appealing. I see us swimming in the hotel pool, going to the beach, having sex, writing, as if we were foreign correspondents out of *The Quiet American*. England is not far away enough from that place. I need to be flung further to avoid the temptation of return. I could go for a few days while Gabriel is on his painting retreat in Wales. This brave talk masks my fear of being alone. All my self-destructive tendencies rise to the surface when you take your hand away from mine.

London II

∾

■ In the eyes of his first patron, a man named Eddie Marsh, Gertler was the most beautiful angelic Jew. He also thought that Gertler, with that shiny black fringe, was the greatest genius of his age. For many years, nothing was too much, and Eddie Marsh gave everything: money, the keys to his flat on Gray's Inn Fields, bought paintings from Gertler and his friends: Rosenberg, Bomberg, Kramer. And when the war in the trenches came, Marsh did what he could to help Gertler. But the artist was a pacifist, and Marsh was private secretary to Winston Churchill.

And then, a letter from Gertler: *Since the war, you have gone in one direction and I in another. We are too different now to continue this friendship.*

■ The morning after we get back from Brighton, Gabriel and I arrange to meet on Theobold's Road outside 5 Raymond Buildings, the block where Eddie Marsh lived. The plan,when Gabriel finally arrives (he's late), is to walk from Eddie's flat, then across Bloomsbury to Ottoline's place on Gower Street. I want to get a sense of what it was like to move in Gertler's London.

Last week, on a tour around the East End, the guide had met us outside Aldgate Station and led us along Petticoat Lane, onto Leyden Street, pointing out the underground toilets – the Petticoat Lane Parliament – where market traders gathered for political debates. Now the toilets are the local cottage off Wentworth Street, where Gabriel had rented a room for a few month before being hounded out by stall-holders who'd marked his door with spray paint: FUCK OFF POOFTE.

The guide took us to Gertler's place on Elder Street, talked about the predatory homosexuals (Eddie Marsh, for example) who fell in love with Gertler, this beautiful man, a bit of East End rough.

"These were the slums, after all" the guide tells us, visibly excited by his own gossip.

And there was Ottoline Morell, she too a voracious sex fiend. Spittle forms at the edges of his mouth. Her husband – there's more, as if showing us dirty pictures – the most cuckolded man in England.

In the early 1900s, in the days of revolution and anarchy, when the Brick Lane Mosque was the Spitalfields Great Synagogue, Gertler and others – crowds of them – would gather on Yom Kippur to watch the anarchists throw ham and cheese sandwiches at the *shul*. Our guide talks about the gentrification of the area, about the rich Jews who'd moved out and wanted nothing to do with restoration or preservation. At the end of the tour, in the pub, he tells us about a gang of Bangladeshi boys who petrol-bomb the white pubs, ransack the churches, rip the pulpits from the floor and steal the silver.

"And," he says. "if you want to teach these people English, they call you a rashist."

"But..."

"Don't," Gabriel says.

It's an awkward moment, the guide lost somewhere in the fragmented continuum of Whitechapel history, unsure where to position himself. Caught between the sadness of his own predicament and the ghosts of the Jewish East End. And I wonder, as we sit quietly – shocked and bemused – sipping our tonic water, if those of us who are obsessed with the past, who find meaning and substance by fiddling with history, if our attempts to resuscitate the dead are a search for metaphors to give meaning to our grief and guilt and loneliness.

And here I stand outside Eddie Marsh's building as Gertler must have stood countless times, inhaling deeply as he prepared to ask for something. Can I borrow... can I have... would you please... Then a text from Gabriel to say he's on the bus, that last night's life-drawing group went on for longer than expected. They'd gone for a drink and he'd drunk too much. *I'll be with u in 5. I have a surprise.*

This gives me time to take notes about the long wide driveway in front of Raymond Buildings, the white facade, the solid doorway of Number 5. A plaque with the names of the barristers who work upstairs. Behind me, people in suits and pressed skirts pass back and forth from Theobold's Road to I'm not sure where.

"Can I help?" a man says.

In his mid-fifties, dark hair, smart, relaxed in the way rich people often are. He clearly belongs in the building, a barrister from upstairs. There is nothing suspecting about him, he's not afraid of intruders. I tell him I'm writing a book, that the painter Mark Gertler stayed here, upstairs, in the top floor flat owned by a man called Edward Marsh.

"That's where we live," he says.

As if Eddie Marsh was right there.

Gertler, too.

As easy as that. As coincidental.

And up we go.

■ What's now the dining room was Eddie's bedroom. The study, where the barrister keeps his pipe collection, was Mrs Elgy's room. Marsh redid the flat to maximise the wall space so that he could hang paintings everywhere. The barrister shows me the fireplace that was here back then, next to it, a brown Labrador lifts its head – it looks tired, like it has lived for too long already. Upstairs, the daughter is home from school, her room used to be the kitchen, Delft tiles on the wall behind her bed.

"He's writing a book about Eddie Marsh," he tells her.

After Marsh and Gertler had fallen out over Eddie's support of the war – *this misery that separates everyone like darkness* – there was no way they could see eye to eye. *I have come to the conclusion*, Gertler wrote, *that we had better not meet any more, and I can no longer accept your help.* Eddie had always made him feel welcome, no matter when he turned up, no matter how little notice he gave, no matter what he asked for and what he refused. *This is your home.* There was the seduction. There were limits. But the war was the final straw. It was a way to end things nobly. Gertler would always be grateful, always remember the debt he could never repay, he'd miss Marsh for his unconditional giving. His was the first grand home Gertler had been invited into, the first away from Spital Square and Elder Street, the first that softened everything with thick carpets and wide armchairs.

■ "What's the matter?" he said.

Eddie stood above him early one morning, there in the living room in his dressing gown and slippers, as if shocked into silence. His voice a whisper.

"Men," he said. "Such beautiful men."

"Should I leave?" Gertler said.

"I was watching you in the bath," Eddie said. "I shouldn't have."

"What did you see?"

"I saw myself as a boy," Eddie said. "I was eight or nine, timid, getting ready to swim in the lake."

"And?" said Gertler.

"I don't wish to alarm you."

"Tell me."

"An older boy was standing next to me, my head level with his chest. As if it was the most casual thing in the world, he removed his bathing suit and there it was, an epiphany, like a gift, this thick mound of hair. It wasn't his penis that stunned, but the lusciousness of that dark patch in the centre of his body."

"Carrington has a dark patch," Gertler said.

"Must you?"

"She'd rather have a penis," he said. "Anything to please the old poof."

Eddie straightened his tie. Breakfast was almost ready.

"I remember thinking," Eddie said. "There couldn't be anything as wonderful as that knoll of plumage and the fishbone of hair that rises from its edges."

"And then what?" Gertler said.

"And then there you were," said Eddie. "Stepping out of the bath. Exactly like that boy. And you carried on talking to me, chatting away in that casual manner you have, as if nothing out of the ordinary was happening."

"I like it when you look."

Gertler could see himself through the other man's eyes, slouched in the armchair, legs outstretched, flushed from the hot water, hair damp and dark. He undid the cord of his dressing gown, opened it for Eddie to see his pale chest and stomach, for his gaze to follow the trickle of hair that ran down from his belly-button.

"You are so perfect."

"Sh," said Gertler. "Think of what you couldn't do, how quickly you turned away."

"Stop," Eddie said, picking up his briefcase, heading straight for the Houses of Parliament.

■ "We love the view," the barrister says.

The lawns of Gray's Inn Fields, benches, oak trees, clerks and secretaries on a mid-morning break, thinking of work drinks later that evening, of birthday gifts to buy, places to escape to in the summer, and there's always someone writing a poem, planning a novel, a story that wants to be told, something they've been carrying around for a long time.

I will remember very little of all this, these minutes I spend here, the brief time it takes to show me the flat.

This was this, this was that, this was where... And then the barrister walks me down the stairs and out onto the wide private driveway. We have the same problem as they did back then, he says: coming into the driveway at night after the gates have been shut.

He'd bought the flat from the people who'd bought the flat from Eddie Marsh, touched the hand that touched the hand that touched Gertler. And now, as we shake, I am included in the chain.

"If you ever need to come back," he says.

But I never do. And for some reason, when Gabriel turns up, suitcase on wheels, ready for his painting trip to Wales, I tell him nothing of what has just happened.

"I was telling the homos about you," he says, luggage trailing behind as we exit the gates and walk up Theobald's Road. "I've discovered the son."

"What son?"

"Gertler's son."

"His grave?"

"He lives with his boyfriend in West London."

"Who told you this?"

"People who know people."

"Tell me."

"I like teasing you," he says.

"I'll smack you."

"I like that, too," he says. "I've been thinking, we should do more of that. I want to do the things you like."

"Focus," I say.

"Someone in the life-drawing group knows all sorts of people, goes to dinner parties. A couple of weeks ago he went to Luke Gertler's place."

"You mean the real son of Mark Gertler?"

"Do you want to meet him?"

"I thought he was dead."

"Do you?"

Gabriel hands me a scrap of paper with the name of Mark Gertler's son on it, and beneath it, a phone number.

Because now, ready or not, something is about to happen, something that could change the course of everything. I'm seeing glimpses of the dead, flesh of their flesh. There are places we don't go to because we don't know they're there. What if we were provided with every avenue available to increase the scope of our world? Would we say yes? Heading towards Ottoline's house, Gabriel's hand in mine. I'm still not sure how I feel about a companion on this journey, this trip to Hades that should be done alone. I am Orpheus, the musician who wants to stare death in the face. I ought to warn you: If you wait a while, I'll regret everything, even the day we met. Stop trying to tempt me with your naked body, exposing your bits. I'll turn my robe into a pool of clear water, draw you in and fake my own drowning, anything to mask the violence of my disappearance. I will dye the scene crimson. But wait... listen... is that a flute I hear on the other side of the fence? Is that the howling of beasts? Watch me run. Watch my silk scarf and taffeta gown billow in the wind. I have destructive powers the likes of which you cannot imagine. The flute, I hear it, the flute and the shrieking of animals. You can't catch me. I'm on my way to the dead, one step at a time down the spiral staircase.

"Careful," Gabriel says. "The light's red."

Holding me back while the cars speed by.

"You saved my life," I say.

"Hardly," he says. "But you can owe me anyway."

Somewhere in the world it's getting colder. A war is raging, a child is being sold for cash or raped or infected by HIV. A person talks about being shot, lifts her trouser leg, her dress, the hem of her skirt to reveal a scar where a bullet has entered. We all want evidence of our survival, to share the marks that life has left on our skin: the accidents, mistakes. These scars are where something went wrong, then healed. Spring is just around the corner.

Part 2

London III

స్

■ A few years ago, for a while, Kevin and I dated. It wasn't a success. We did the whole domestic thing, pretended to be a couple, cooked and shopped and went to a gay pub near his flat in Tottenham. We watched a lot of TV. The sex was good. We liked each other, but not enough to keep the happy-couple thing going. In less than six months, it was over. While Gabriel is in Wales, Kevin comes over for sex. His new boyfriend is not very adventurous when it comes to sex. He'd die if he found out he was here.

"Then why do it?" I say.

"It's about me," he says.

"But you could mess it up."

"I know," he says. "I'm taking a risk."

After a couple of whiskies – Kevin's with ice, mine with honey, lemon and boiling water (I'm coming down with something) – we go to bed. That's what he's here for and I'm the service provider. I'm not complaining. I get off on being this creation: a mock top, a man-made pleasurer of bottoms.

"My cock's staying hard for longer than usual," I say.

"Keep it that way," he says.

■ Every evening in the tavern owned by the Gertlers on the outskirts of a village in Poland, fights break out between Mr Gertler and the drunken soldiers. Coarse and rosy-cheeked, young and cruel, they behave like marauding locusts. Gertler watches his parents freeze with cold sweat, ferry out liquor and food. The evenings are full of anxiety, at times so forceful Gertler thinks he'll choke, that he'll never wake from these loud raw nights. The soldiers insist on playing with the boy, dressing him in a uniform made especially by the tailor at the garrison, epaulettes and stars, so that he can parade up and down, stand to attention, and the soldiers salute back, cheer, then call for more drinks. His mother never denies the *goyim* their mascot, the mascot that is her own son.

And so his love of performing is born, his desire to walk into a room and be liked: as long as the *goyim* are laughing, as long as they're in their seats and smiling, he is safe. It was an ugly time back then. he was a baby when they left England and returned to the spleen of Europe, the father schlepping them to Poland, making a mess of things again – the inn business, the boots and button stall in the market. Eventually he buggered off to America and left the family to fend for themselves.

The mother wails: "*Oi vei iz mir*," nightly, a chorus of one, home from the restaurant she worked at, her payment in left-overs: food for the children's supper. "What a life! *Nor tsores. Tsores*! And *farvos*? Come write a letter, Maxale. Write to your *tutalla*."

So he sits there, all four years old of him, chin level with the table to draw his first picture, a wish, the thing he wants brought from America. The eagerness with which he holds the pen, as if the thing itself were food, wood to gnaw on, ink to gulp down. Slowly, deliberately, precisely: an apple. Then another and another.

"Papa bring this."

Then he adds a bowl.

Five years after trying to make it in Przemysl, the mother and her five children head back to London. The father is hopeful: "Come," he writes from America. "I have prospects. We shall meet in England." And then on the boat – boat!? You call this a boat! *Nu*, so on the cattleship back to London, Gertler dances at the first sound of music. It's enough for the wind to blow against the mast for the child to be up on his feet in that orange coat with its gold and scarlet braid, vermilion tam-o-shanter, knee-high boots, and the crew and passengers and his very own people can't get enough of him. Any minute now and he'll be lifting off into thin air.

Of his father he remembers very little: not the colour of his eyes, his smell, not the sound of his voice, though he hears it sometimes in his brothers. He doesn't remember the beatings, nor loving the man while he was growing up, as if early on they'd given up on each other. Later, he'd learn to align himself with men like Eddie Marsh who'd provide for him, buy his paintings. He remembers the arguments, accusations, the intensity of hate, the sulking of his mother.

"Without you, Maxale..." she would say.

Him she loved more than anything.

Call me Maxale – he said to Carrington, but she couldn't produce his name in any fashion close to his mother's, for our mouths are shaped by others to make certain sounds, to move our lips and tongues in certain ways. These are the stories with which we enter the world, passed down through blood. Let's face it, go back as far and as wide as you like, you're not going to find not a single *farkakte* Yiddisher amongst the Carringtons.

■ When he stops for the night in Dover and calls Marjorie from the Rembrandt Hotel, she tells him that Carrington is dead. While he crossed the Channel she killed herself. He knew she'd follow Lytton.

"Will you come straight back to London?" Marjorie says.

"I could head to the South of France," he says.

"Don't," she says, as if she knows how that journey could end.

In the dark of the hotel's dining room, a strip of light under the closed door. What will he do now that the one he wants has gone? The one to whom he wrote love letters without restraint or shame. Love is a one-sided thing, reciprocity the exception. It's not often you get to love someone and that someone loves you back. I'm not sure I've ever had that. I've loved deeply and been loved, mostly not at the same time, and if at the same time, the extent was never the same, neither the duration. One person always stops before the other.

■ Then on Friday, the German comes over. I've never been with a German, my foray into the tribal embargo. We spoke on the phone and even though his voice grated on me, I'd said: "That would be nice." And thought to myself: *You're on a roll. Run with it.* He cycled down from Stamford Hill, not as handsome as I'd expected, but handsome enough and he brings his bike in and we shake hands. We sit in the kitchen and talk about "arriving" – he calls it the sense of arrival when I tell him how it feels to be forty. How it feels to more or less know who you are and what you want from life, to have direction, to stop experimenting with other callings.

"Yes," he says. "You've arrived."

"I don't usually think of myself as that," I say. "But

when you put it like that, it feels like it could be true."

There are times when we feel big in a person's presence, when the quality of their listening, the honesty of their being there – their *hakshava* (there's something Talmudic about that word: *hakshava*) – when their *hakshava* is honest and open and engaged. But still, I hold back, because I always do, and yet I talk more than usual: about coming to London, about living in Israel, about its compulsive re-enactment of the Holocaust drama and other persecution plotlines. It's not often I feel listened to so intently. Do we only talk when we feel listened to, or do we talk (write) *in order* to get someone to listen?

(Are you listening?)

The German says he's lived in fifty different places in eight countries. His mother has kept every letter he's sent. London, he says, has been the hardest. And while he talks I scan his arms, the redness of his fingertips, his neck, the way his face seems too chiselled, like someone who is ill. I want to ask him what it feels like to have his body waste away like this.

"What are you thinking?" he says.

"I was thinking whether we should go to bed."

He says our meeting has been like a gift and he doesn't want to spoil it. He says sex would ruin the energy that flows between us. Let's keep in touch, he says. And yet, when he gets up to leave and we stand at the door, and kiss, my heart (a cliché) jumps a beat. We kiss gently, cautious of the wild animals that lurk in our mouths, the ones that lie in wait for the zebras at the edge of the lake.

Ogres in the caverns of our mouths.

When your tongue licks my teeth.

And then he is gone.

■ Those who shot and killed and destroyed and wounded and maimed and stole and debased, have reason to be silent. How do you speak of the horrors you committed if there's neither judge nor jury? What do you say when no one expects you to say anything, to recount your deeds. What we saw... should we not be talking of this? And really, if you think about it, if I think about it, if anyone thinks about it – *think about it!* – how different are we, what difference is there between the ones who did and the ones who didn't? I'm not only talking about Lebanon in 1982, not only about Israel. I don't need a chorus here, a choir of penitents. All I want is to tell the story of what I saw, what I saw one person do, and then the death, the death and the cleaning up and the resumption of daily life.

And if the Gertlers had stayed in Europe? If they had kept trying to make it there, destitute, persecuted by the *goyim*, sitting ducks at pogrom season, all of that until he was in his 30s, his 40s – the right age to be barefoot in the snow digging graves for his brethren, the right age for the gas chambers. Would he have made it to where he made it anyway? Who'd have painted *Merry-Go-Round*? Who'd have loved Carrington as much as he did? Monty and Eddie and Tom would have found other men to love. The son, Luke, would never have made it into the world. And Marjorie, who would she have married? And me, what about me? Who would have kept *me* company? How would all this have existed without Gertler, destined to die at forty-seven, just weeks before the start of the world's second great war?

■ A kitten scampers up the easel and jumps onto Gabriel's shoulder, sits transfixed by the choreography of stroking and marking, then makes a grab for his hand. The brush, the movement itself, kitten leaping from shoulder to canvas, clawing, falling to floor, fur marked by colour of sky.

My mind wanders while Gabriel speaks, my listening not as good as it should be, his voice a background hum, my thoughts turning to mystery's gradual disappearance. I need to be woken with a bang, the caverns of my imagination split open. I want to worry, be moved, have ideas that thrill, conversations, encounters. It's not that I'm losing interest, it's me – I'm beginning to wonder what the point of my existence is. I don't want to drain him of whatever he needs to keep painting. I can't elaborate – there's too much to say. I need a battalion at my back to stay alive – a force that will carry me. Either that, or let me set out on this expedition alone, pen and paper in hand.

When Gabriel and I are done talking, I make the call.

"This is Luke Gertler."

"I'm writing a book about your father."

A soft, open voice, a gentleness that is both vulnerable and assured, a man who has been in the world for many years. It would take a lot to phase him. I wasn't expecting such ease.

"I'd like to talk to you?" I say.

"I have some of his paintings," he says.

"I'd love to see them," I say.

"When would be convenient?"

■ Peter walks over from the other side of Finsbury Park. We'd been chatting on Gaydar. Only when we're in the kitchen do we realise we know each other from a poetry course we did together at Morley College.

"I was disappointed when you stopped coming," I say.

He sits with his elbows on the table, head in hands. I walk behind him to get milk from the fridge for our tea, and put my palm on his head, stroke his hair. It is soft and straight and long. Back then, all semester, I had wanted to touch him.

"I'm sorry," he says. "I can't have sex with people

I've had a conversation with."

I want to laugh, but he looks troubled. He's trying to work out which place is best for him, Malaga or here. If he stays in Spain he'll miss London, though as time goes by he misses it less, but when he's here it's always for some practical reason, always for a brief stay, never long enough to actually settle back in.

"Take soap, for example," he says. "I'm here for a week in my flat and I didn't have any soap and I thought: Is it really worth buying soap for just a couple of days?"

"You've been washing without soap?"

"I had a bath this evening," he says.

"Without soap?" I say.

"I'm a lost cause," he says. "My boyfriends are always leaving me."

His nails are dirty brown crescents, a boy just in from digging graves for hamsters, ready for a good scrub.

The Colombian waiter left him for a Turkish dancer. Then he dated a Basque guy, also a waiter, twenty years older than him. The older man had a small flat on the beach and Peter had moved in with him, but they had separate bedrooms so the older guy could bring his lovers home for the night. Peter had an affair with an Italian guy he met on the beach while he was still living with the old man, who eventually left him for an English tourist.

I, too, want an array of characters in my story, more than just me and Gabriel and the occasional fuck on the side. I want intrigue and jealous rages and the slamming of doors. I want what Peter's got, a kind of destitution that drags strangers into its orbit, that reads like a Mexican soap opera, the kind of story that's clearly hopeless from the start, and yet you have to keep watching, clinging to your faith in a happy ending.

"I'm a real shit," Peter says. "Trust me, you don't want to have sex with me."

But I do. I want to feel there is something in me that can save you, come to your rescue, understand you, take away your sadness.

"We could cuddle," I say. "Just lie in bed and talk."

While I kiss my way down Peter's chest and stomach, a gang of Arsenal supporters walks past, chanting. He turns towards the window, stares out at the sky, a rough sea-storm of grey clouds. It's getting dark, a hazy city-night kind of darkness, but I don't want to switch on the bedside lamp. We listen to the next-door neighbour in her kitchen clanging pots, opening drawers, closing cupboards, like a hungry child signalling for company: it's time for the grown-ups to stop doing what they're doing and feed me. Buses pass, more Arsenal fans march by singing something to the tune of "The German officers crossed the line." I stroke the side of his body, the curve from ribs to hip. It's like we're marooned somewhere, here in bed on the top floor, windows open and sounds coming in from outside. Eventually he gets up to leave.

We do not touch or shake hands. No hug, no kisses, no nothing.

■ Gabriel is chatty during our late-night conversation. Things are going well in Wales. I'm not used to this kind of positivity, a jubilant kind of bubbliness, child-like, trusting, a telling that is sure of its listener. It scares me. It's an affront, an entire rugby team, five-a-side football, a line of Haka dancers calling out to me and all I want is to sulk on the sidelines, revel in my ambivalent desire to join in. Gabriel tells me there's a writer in the house finishing a biography of some crazy Chilean poet.

"A poet in love with her cousin," he says. "She wrote all these letters to him. She'd never even met the guy."

"Did she know the poet?" I say.

"Who?" he says.

"The writer," I say. "Did she know the poet?"

"I don't know," he says. "Is that important?"

"Tell me more about the poet," I say.

From her balcony, she'd spy on the young man she was besotted with while he made out with his girlfriend in the courtyard. One day, out of frustration, she began tearing roses off the climbing bushes and threw petals onto the lovers, handful after handful, ripping at the petals, thorns clawing at her skin.

"Do you keep your love letters?" I say.

"I don't have any," Gabriel said.

"None?"

"Do you?" he said.

There'd been a time, not so long ago, last year, perhaps, when I considered burning all the letters I've been carrying with me, a box of them, accumulated since I was a teenager. I'd opened the box hoping that stories would rise to the surface, that my past would inspire me, words triggering narratives, conjuring up landscapes. But none of that happened. Some things were not there in the letters, things I'd not written to anyone about, things no one referred to, mainly to do with the war back in the 1980s.

"Are you listening?" Gabriel says. "I was talking about you last night."

"I want a letter from you," I say.

"*You* write to *me*," he says.

"I wrote from Sitges," I say. "But never sent it."

"Send it now. Or write me a new one."

"You'll be back in a few days," I say.

"Do you miss me?" he says.

Don't pause.

"Of course I do."

■ For her sake, Gertler would keep going. His entire being had once depended on her. You're my brother, she'd said. And here he was, going over letters, reading what had been written fifteen years ago, a mad love, revisiting who he was, not so different from now, not so different from what Carrington must have felt, robbed of her beloved, watching Lytton succumb to cancer and die in bed.

He'd written to say how shocked he was that Lytton's end had come so early. What an enormous blow it must be. There was little one could say on such an occasion, but he'd hoped she'd muster the strength and courage to go on and rebuild a purpose in life. He had one or two letters and poems from Lytton that he could show her when she felt ready. Meanwhile, all my love and best wishes.

His last words to her.

All my love and best wishes. Mark.

■ Their house is near the end of a road that opens onto a green. I'm concerned about the lack of fiction in such a meeting, worried about the restrictions something as concrete as a living relative – the son himself – could put on my entire project. The dead are easier to manipulate. This meeting could coerce me into being more factual, or feel guilty for not being: I'd have to think twice before fiddling with the facts of Mark Gertler's life and death. Would I still, after meeting his flesh and blood, this man in his seventies who was once a boy receiving news of his father's suicide, would I still be able to make

Gertler do things he didn't do, say things he never said, go places he may never have been? And the sex with Carrington – what about that? – in all its desperate and clumsy detail, and the scene with Eddie Marsh about to touch him, and the weeks in Sitges, the days in France, the frustration with Marjorie, the approaching moment of disappearance?

So I decided, in the seconds it took for Luke Gertler's boyfriend to open the front door, that whatever was said and done and seen after the door opened would appear in this book. I was ready to step inside with curiosity and kindness, but without scruples. I would get from Luke Gertler whatever he had to give that no one else could give, the kind of things only a son would know.

The entrance hall is covered in framed illustrations from children's books, scenes of adventure and discovery, idyllic settings, a lone tree in a field, a young boy fishing on a boat on a lake, a dog asleep at its master's feet. Then I'm ushered into the living room to meet the son of the man I'm writing about. He's handsome, tall, unguarded, and when, much later, when I leave, when the tea and tour and the things that will happen between us have happened, when I'm back at the front door and we hug, I will think: he is solid, the painter's son is sturdy, so different from his father, the pretty one, skinny, light enough to lift from the floor and carry to bed.

We drink tea from china cups. Me, the painter's son and his boyfriend, the man he has lived with for twenty years. They offer me tea-cakes wrapped in purple foil, fruitcake from Christmas, a slice of stollen from friends in Berlin. I'm perched on the edge of my armchair, too nervous to lean back. I feel I should be sitting with my knees together, balancing the cup and saucer on my lap. The father's paintings take up most of the wall space: trees at Banchory, a still life with chrysanthemums, an old man with a beard. On the shelves and dressers, an army of Staffordshire pottery: a cavalier on horseback, mallard ducks, figurines of white, pastel blues and pinks, not the kind of thing you'd expect to see in the home of a twenty-first-century homosexual.

"Do you paint?" the son says.

"I took some classes when I began the book," I say.

"We must show him Roger's drawings," the boyfriend says.

"Would you like to see some photographs?"

It's surreal, this being here in a room with Gertler's son, the fruit of his loins, his paintings on the walls, a macabre reminder of the man who killed himself. Our conversation is stilted. The painter's son looks at me in a way I've been looked at by older men, men who've been looking at men for a long time. When I comment that he doesn't look like his father, the boyfriend tells the story of how they met through friends who'd invited them for dinner. I tell them about Gabriel, about where we met, about him being a painter. I tell them that there are days when he is everything I ever wanted, and days when I just want to be alone.

"We like that sauna," the painter's son says. "Don't we?"

I'm in the middle, holding the photo album, half of it resting on the son's lap, the other half on mine. In one photograph Gertler is naked on all fours, like a cat, bum in the air. For someone like me, who likes my men slim and smooth, Mark Gertler is what I like. I can imagine what poor, frustrated Monty Sherman must have been thinking, sitting there on the beach with a small blanket over his hard-on while Gertler frolicked in the sand.

"Is that your mother?" I say.

"That was after he died," says the son.

"What drew them together?" I say.

"Physical attraction," the boyfriend says.

I do not mention Carrington. I do not mention the men who fell in love with his father. It's as if all this might be gossip he's unaware of, maybe he hasn't been told, as if I'm the first to ever pay him a visit. I don't mention how beautiful Gertler is, or the fact that I'm a stranger in a house looking at someone's father's bum, then at his wife, the woman some blamed for his death.

"She never uttered a harsh word about him," Luke says, and tells me how he'd sit in his mother's kitchen while she cooked, sometimes helping her bake a cake, asking, over and over, for the story of how his father liked sweet things, how he could barely fry an egg and would eat anything put in front of him, always insisting on dessert.

"Have another biscuit," the son says.

■ Five years after his father killed himself, Luke was living in France with Marjorie and her new boyfriend, Franz, an Austrian refugee. They spoke French to each other, especially when the Nazis were around. This was during the occupation and death camps were an option for people like Luke.

"When we got back to England," he says. "I couldn't speak a word of English."

As if the boy who'd been sent to a sanatorium, thin and sickly, the boy they feared might be a consumptive like his father, as if that boy is still here, sitting on the sofa beside me, the air of someone not from here, made delicate and fragile by displacement. Perhaps that is what suicide does to the children of the dead – leaves them in a constant state of grief and bafflement.

"We go back to that house in France every summer," Luke says.

"She left it to us when she died," the boyfriend says.

"We've built a wall around the courtyard."

"You should come," his boyfriend says.

"He likes hairy men," Luke says.

The boyfriend smiles.

"I think he wants to show you Roger's drawings."

The painter's son and I sit in silence, two men quietly awkward amongst the pottery figurines: a farm-boy leaning against a gate, a row of bone-china cottages. I'm beginning to wonder if I really want to be here, if I really do have to talk to people to tell the story in the way I want to. We could journey back to the past, revel in our shared fascination with the father, tell the story of how it really was. I ask about Gertler's friends, whether Luke is still in contact with their families. What about the Rosenbergs? The Bombergs? Does he have any contact with them? Not really, but he has a poem that Rosenberg wrote and gave to his father, a sonnet scribbled down during one of their life-drawing classes at the Slade.

"I think he's found Roger's book," Luke says. "Shall we go and see?"

■ The whiteness of the room, pale grey pyjamas, beige cardigan, the nurse's starched uniform tight against her plumpness, the doctor's overcoat, the linen – everything! – in all that whiteness, from somewhere: the smell of toast, tea brewing, egg whites crisping at the edges – in the distance... it's a dream... something... Marjorie in the back garden on a cast iron chair, knees together, arms at her sides, poised to say something, palms pressed to her body. His ghost tiptoes across the paving stones, his presence like coal dust, the sound of bees.

"Mark," she says.

In 1936 he was back at Mundesley, the lost body. When tumbleweed starts to roll it rolls, blown across plains, pausing and turning. The movement never ends. That's what grief is: a constant fluctuation. My hair is grey and my eyes black pebbles. I could waste away in minutes.

"You will not leave me like this," she says.

As if the last ten years have been spent in a dank cluttered bunker, heavy-footed soldiers overhead. But enough. It's time to go from bondage to freedom, from darkness to light, from anger to joy. This story of hunger is no longer interesting. The story that is hunger, the artist's skin and burden. For brief moments – look, it's about to happen! – the hunger will disappear, not because he has eaten, but because he's about to start painting, so furiously he won't even notice the grumbling inside.

"I want to go home," he says.

"Let me get your shoes," she says.

"We should be going to Paris," he says.

"Your breakfast, Mr Gertler," the nurse with the tray.

The garden is a spectrum of greens, everything lush and wet from the rain. A grand manor house rather than a sanatorium. On the veranda beneath his window, the shoots in the terracotta pots are sprouting leaves, nature in all its generosity. Now, after the nurse has brought him an apple and some toast, he prepares for his hour of painting.

■ We huddle together around pencil drawings of naked men: an old man getting his cock sucked, a lumberjack in the woods with his trousers at his ankles, drops of sweat in his chest hair, a drawing-room scene with a gentleman in an armchair by the window, shirt unbuttoned, nipples corpulent, and in the doorway behind him, a naked butler with a tray of sherry.

"Before you go," Luke says. "I want to give you some postcards."

Over the roofs of the houses opposite, a bright and cloudless sky, as if we were somewhere else, away from the gloom of London, a blank canvas. In the silence of a room a clock ticks, the tapping of time, inexorable. I don't want to see the poem by Rosenberg, nor the other photo albums, nor the paintings in the kitchen. I don't want to be so close to the dead. I want Gabriel, his body, our state of living.

■ The day before Gabriel gets back from Wales I'm in Room 19 at Tate Britain, standing before Gertler's *Merry-Go-Round. Your terrible and beautiful painting*, Lawrence had written. *The first picture you have ever painted.* A carousel turning, faces petrified, ninety years and their throats still parched. The carnival noise in the background, tinny music, a moth circling a flame, oxen tethered to the grindstone. Back then in 1916 in his studio, a short walk from the Heath, its merriment on weekends, miles from his family in Whitechapel, he worked on his *Merry-Go-Round* to make sure it was ready for the London Group exhibition. At night he followed the searchlights for Zeppelins. Soon the bombs will fall. War then and war now, this insane war that began weeks ago in Palestine and the one that began just after his death, war that led to the Promised Land and now to the bombing of Gaza.

Painting as tombstone and bond. Scarlet, crimson, Prussian blue, white, a stained-glass window, frozen sounds. Closer up, the brush-strokes are visible, each a gift, transitions between colours, red to orange, blue to white, the marks of his hand, and because no one is here in the gallery room, I approach the painting and, careful not to wake the dead, stroke its surface with my fingertips.

■ A man takes his seat at the vacant table, eats soup from a bowl, drinks a banana smoothie. A slice of quiche is cut up and devoured. The plate – just like that – empty. The final spoonfuls of soup swallowed in a hurry, the smoothie downed in quick gulps, brief pauses between each.

Still Life with Man, Quiche, and Banana Smoothie.
Empty Chairs
A Cup
A Plate
A White Bowl

A waiter comes to clear, tilting his body to expose a slither of flesh between shirt and belt. Trousers snug against pert round bum. I finish my nut roast and broccoli. When the waiter returns to take my empty plate, I lift my glass of water for him to spray and wipe, starting at the centre, working outwards, pencil-marks of thin hair on his arm, circles growing wider and wider until he is wiping along the rim, leaving trails of moisture behind, shining.

"What are you reading?" he says.

What does one say about Vasari's *Lives of the Artists*?

"Are you an artist?" I say.

"Broadly speaking," he says.

I can tell when I'm about to get involved (yes, it does have the word "love" hidden in it). Fernando is thirty-seven, from Portugal. We catch the Tube back to Finsbury Park and go straight to bed. We don't make it to the living room. If we need water, there's a bottle by the bed. He strokes my chest.

"I've never seen so much hair," he says.

"You're so smooth," I say.

He barely has any pubic hair, or hair under his arms.

"Turn over," he says, and runs his fingers across my back.

"That feels nice," I say.

His hands are warm against my skin. Suddenly I want to sleep, to lie close together.

"What do you do?" I say.

"I'm a painter," he says. "I studied in Paris."

"I'm going to Paris next week," I say.

"I love Paris."

"Do you know the *Merry-Go-Round*?" I say.

"What's that?"

"The carousel," I say. "The painting with the people shouting. Room 19."

"You like that painting?" he says.

Our lovemaking is slow and intense, the kind that makes you feel that, yes, you could fall in love. I'm here and Gabriel's there and I don't know what he's doing, this crime of being with someone else, of really being with someone, of sharing the bed we share, of opening my mouth to another, breathing into each other's lungs, like this, in and out, passing air back and forth, our bodies pressed together so that our breathing is one, and the body, my body, as it makes its way into his, to assume his skin, as he pushes back, asking for more

and more

and more

"What time do you need to get up?" he says.

"I don't," I say.

"Me neither," he says.

■ The nurse at his bedside quietly turns the pages of the Picasso book, the sound of her fingers against paper, lifting a page, laying it flat, smoothing it with her palm. He'd seen the excitement in her face, that enthusiasm to be inspired, to know... her eyes – questions. He'd provide and she'd blossom. The sheet pulled up to his neck, his body shrouded. It's easier not to say anything, to be without the expectation of speech. Keep your eyes closed, breathe slowly, as if you're calm and rested. He wants night's insulation, turning windows into walls, his room detaching itself from the world.

Painting exhausted him, as did the waning of interest in his work. Friends encouraged him to keep writing, but he stopped after the chapter on his depression, his words becoming cerebral, stiff. He wasn't used to being confined to one colour. He hardly ever used black – he'd learnt this from the French – and now they want the *ganse megilah* in monochrome! One stick of charcoal, one nib of gall ink. Where's the mess, the moving around? The colour!

Waiting is what he does best. It's not just him, two thousand years of suffering are about to come to an end, the Jews are about to sound the death-cry that will ripple through the generations. Isn't that what Lawrence had said in his letter? How could anyone paint under such circumstances? Sometimes he thinks it's the return journey home. He'd be the first to admit fear, so he does nothing, wallows in poverty. Money from the four paintings will have to last a year. Is that even possible? And if he did have enough, what would he do?

Give him sunshine, heat, let him melt, become paint.

The page turning has stopped: she could be asleep with the book in her lap. He listens for clues. She hasn't moved in ten, fifteen, twenty minutes. It's hard to tell when you're weak and fed-up and tired and the birds are quietly chirping and the wind rustles in the trees and the world seems to be holding its breath.

■ "Was I snoring?"

Fernando stands in the doorway, a man I hardly know, tall and slim, nothing between his skin and air. It's hard to be precise about what I feel: a mixture of gratitude, arousal, a willingness to give everything away, to give it all up. To stop writing. To become a thing reliant on sensual gratification. I also know I am not what he wants, I will never be the kind of man he'll love. I demand and expect. Nothing is ever enough, except in those moments when we're naked and all there is is the body.

"Come back to bed," he says.

"I need to write a bit more," I say. "I don't want to

forget any of this."

"Of what?"

"Us," I say.

A street cleaner drags a broom along the pavement, the light from streetlamps reflects off his thick golden necklace. A second street-cleaner, older and balder, spade in hand, lugs a plastic bin behind him on a rope. A fat couple in matching tracksuits waddles up the road. These streetlamps are new – brighter than the old ones – still, my window is high enough to avoid their direct light.

When I'm finished writing... how rare to be able to say: I've written all I can, the ink flowing from the tips of my fingers, no distinction between nib and skin, as if biro blue emerged from inside me, an untangling of thread, line after line, left to right, left to right, winding my way down the page – I long for a conversation with Gabriel, and my heart sinks – yes, that too, there is such a thing, he so far from here, there in Wales, light years away. From the day he stepped into this flat, it has felt like it was meant to be. I don't want to keep having the bed to myself, to come home to an empty house. What would it be like to really let go, to step into the whatever of intimacy?

Back in bed, I pull the duvet up over both of us and Fernando turns away from me so that I can wrap myself around him.

■ The bulrushes in the pond are growing back, their stalks jutting out of the water, the plum tree flaunts its white blossoms, the apple tree sprouts green shoots, a dome of purple lobelia grows out of the wall. Then, from the thicket of bulrushes, as if on cue, a duck and her ducklings appear – five, six – travelling in single file behind the mother as if tied by a piece of string, gliding in the path she creates through the algae on the surface, a path that closes immediately behind the last duckling. Once they get back to the nest where Gertler is standing, the ducklings disperse to play on their own: one lifts its body out of the water and flaps its wings, then climbs onto a ledge at the side of the pond. Once up, it can't get down. On the edge of the tiny jetty, looking down, moving its wings.

Jump, Gertler thinks, it's only water. You'll bob back up to the surface.

Branches appear as shadows on the water. Daffodils at the side of the pond, heads heavy on their stems. A goldfish swims below the surface, almost still, its tail a fan of muslin.

Tomorrow he will paint again. He will perch on the window ledge, a bird ready for flight, wings eager and agitated. Trees before him, and below him the safety of the hills, from branch to branch, tree to tree, skimming over water, lifting skywards, heading for the open, the pure blue, no fear when in flight, only the expanse of the heart. I'd rather be up than down, says the bird. There is no limit to anything. What does a bird know of cuddling? How does its vast daily reach effect its need for a cuddle? Those of us who cannot fly, must cuddle. What else is there to do with our wings?

■ Gabriel is crossing the concourse at Euston Station with a man in a white cotton shirt. The man is talking, but Gabriel's eyes are on me, his face lighting up. I want this to be a reunion, for him to smell of home and return and comfort and safety, for his body to reel me in. I want him to be standing here, arms around me, his touch to be the first touch in the morning, his breathing – the last sound at night, to be always this close to one another. But my heart freezes and my body turns cold and the dread of a precious body so close is like death. I want to run back to Fernando, anywhere, to escape. I'd gladly walk off with the man in the white cotton shirt, a man called Peter who shakes my hand and replays a couple of anecdotes from the week in Wales – the mad Chilean poet, a talkative American.

Then Gabriel and I walk towards the bus-stop.

"He tried to seduce me," he says.

"And you said…?"

"No."

"Why?"

"He scares me," Gabriel says.

"Did you tell him?"

"I told him I had a boyfriend," he says.

"Does your boyfriend scare you?"

"Sometimes."

"Like when?"

"Like now," he says.

We stand close together at the bus-stop, my hand in his back pocket, his backside firm and warm. I move the tips of my fingers across it.

"Any news about the book?" he says.

"I spoke to Luke yesterday. He wants to put me in touch with his cousins. He's going to introduce me to Peter Cohen, a big Gertler collector. The Sainsbury family have a few Gertlers. He knows Sarah MacDougall. They want us to come over. They want to meet you. They've invited us to their place in France."

"Did you have sex with them?" Gabriel says.

"Are you serious?"

"I know you," he says.

"I don't want anything to do with him," I say. "It's too confusing."

Our conversations with the dead are private, silent metaphors of our existence, our discoveries ours to keep and hold. Sharing dilutes. The past is God, and what we have to learn from it, from our ancestors – and, really, anyone who came before: dead parents, Gertler, *la même chose*, one a metaphor for the other, and both are metaphors for the choices we make, the kind of life we've chosen... what we learn is already part of the secret make-up of our DNA.

"Here's the bus," Gabriel says.

"I'm glad you're back," I say.

"Me, too," he says.

■ The closer he gets, the further I run. The more open he is, the more my body shuts down. I don't like making love in the dark but today it is the only way to get through it. Pretend he's not Gabriel. Touch his body and imagine he's a stranger, you're in bed with a man who does not know you.

"I don't want to hate you," I say. "I don't want to get to the point where I can't even touch you."

"It sounds like you're already there."

"We can salvage this," I say. "We can find a way to keep going."

"Have you met someone?" he says.

Our lovemaking is brutal, the kind of desperation and abandon I bring to sex with strangers. I wanted to slap him, spit on him. I'd bitten his neck, sucked the blood to the surface, marked him. His fear had hovered in the room after that, and it's here now.

"It felt like you wanted to cross a boundary?"

"What boundary?" I say.

"Between fantasy and what you actually do."

"Most good sex is violent by nature."

"It doesn't have to be."

"I don't have boundaries when it comes to sex," I say. "It's what feels right with each person. Are you talking about the unprotected sex? That was a boundary, and you crossed it too when you came inside me."

"I would never have thought I'd do that."

"But you did," I say.

"I don't want to do that again."

"I trust you," I say.

"You don't," he says. "Trusting that I'm negative is not the same as trusting me as a person, a lover, as someone you can open up to."

"Of course I trust you."

And because it's dark, because it's not Gabriel next to me, because it's him and not him, I don't hold back.

"So," he says. "Who was he?"

"Is," I say. "And there's more than one."

"Do I know them?"

"Of course not," I say. "They're just guys I met."

"Why do you do this?" he says.

"Do what?" I say. "I told you who I am."

"You're not a cruel person," he says. "But you're being cruel. I love you more than that. I know you love me."

"But I can't Gabriel," I say. "I can't."

■ I'd been on guard duty on a Friday afternoon at the entrance to our base near Kfar Qouq in Lebanon. Those who were going home for a long weekend had left already, and those who were staying were in their rooms, sleeping, listening to the radio. In general, the past few weeks had been quieter, now that we were about to withdraw from Lebanon, but still we could be attacked at any minute. The gravel road leading to the guard's hut from the main road was a slalom course of concrete blocks to stop suicide bombers driving into the base. A young man in civilian clothes was walking up the path. Probably from the village, maybe he worked at the grocers, the shop we sometimes went to for Milka and Ritter Sport chocolates.

We were doing guard duty alone by then, even at night. I remember thinking: I'll offer him a cigarette when he gets to the gate. I waved. I might have shouted *salam aleykum* or *bonjour*. I'd like to think I did. For all I knew, he could be from one of the big villas our officers had commandeered for sleeping quarters. I was an intruder in his country.

■ Like mummies in a tomb, Gabriel's breathing soft and measured, his hands clasped on his chest. Strips of light frame the edges of the window-blind, and out of the corner of my eye I watch the outline of him rise and fall. I have felt my heart open before. I know what love feels like, that adrenalin rush, the beating of the heart, the feeling that, yes, it can burst, the heart can beat too fast and burst and cease.

"You have no idea who I am," I say.

"Tell me, my man," he says.

His voice is gentle, and I know there is a film of tears over his eyes.

"I want to know."

He moves closer, turns his body towards mine, his chest touching my arm. It is the kind of body I have always loved, a smooth soft body, a lightness to it, a feeling that it can be lifted and carried and held and clung to. It is a body I have always dreamed of having, a body I didn't know I had when I was younger, a body desired by older men and given to them in the years I gave my body to anyone who asked. Now I am larger, my bulk twice Gabriel's: my body fits around his, like fruit to its core.

"This was more than twenty years ago," I say.

Gabriel puts his hand on my chest and I know that whatever I say, what I'm about to say will be said in the dark, in the blackness that renders everything invisible, a place without witness. I will say what I say and it will not exist when we re-emerge into the light.

"I watched people die," I say. "During the war, I watched."

Every confession is a poem, every honest gesture a lyrical line. That is its strength and dilution. When you've seen war and death, when fear has paralysed you, and still you've survived, then to talk of it is poetry. Every retelling of horror is poetry, the articulation of witnessing. It's the closest we get to transcribing loss.

"I watched and did nothing. That's why I can't bear to be amongst people. I've lost what it means to be human. I saw terrible things, watched and turned away. It's like I've crossed a line."

"We all cross a line," he says. "All it takes is a bit of footage of dead bodies on a roadside, people starving, and we cut to a commercial, or some fucking thing like *The Weakest* fucking *Link*, and that's it, we've crossed a line."

"It's different, though," I say.

"Maybe," he says. "Maybe not."

"It's like death," I say. "So much death, and guilt, and shame. I keep going back, like it's always there, like it's here now, with us, in this room... this place."

"My man," he says, and makes to move closer.

"Don't," I say, because if he touches me, if he leaves his mark on my skin, any imprint of tenderness, I will disappear. "Just sit there," I say.

"I want to know," he says.

"I don't know how," I say. "I don't. I don't know. Will you still..."

"My man," he says.

"Don't," I say.

"I just want to..."

"Don't come closer," I say.

He strokes my chest, barely moving his hand, just his fingers up and down, the tips of his fingers, the kind of gesture that, amplified, could be talons across flesh. He brings his lips to mine, a gentle kiss, no tongues, our mouths tentative.

"You're my first Jewish boyfriend," I say. "Since I left that place."

"Tell me."

"The *goyim* don't get where I'm from. That's why I choose them. But really, their story is also one of watching and doing nothing, of knowing and inaction."

"I'm not sure what to say."

"Don't say anything."

"You didn't kill anyone," he says.

"That isn't it," I say. "I was there. I was there while the killing took place."

"We're all like that," he says. "Everywhere, especially now, here."

"We're going to Paris in a couple of days. All this and we're going to Paris."

"We don't have to go," he says.

"We must," I say. "First the sanatorium at Mundesley, then Paris. Two more trips and Gertler will be dead."

"Then it'll be just you and me," he says.

"Can you handle that?"

"It's not me I'm worried about," he says.

It might seem like I have told him something, that what I said is what I wanted to say, but I've only given him another clue to what I saw, revealed a fraction of the *ganse megillah*, done what criminals and victims of atrocities do, give hints, leave marks, plant seeds and crouch down, wait for lovers to ask questions, to pry, insist on the whole truth. We do not, as the artist said to Gertler, vomit ourselves onto the canvas. Gertler never told them... never told her... his wife... anyone... how much the lack of money was tormenting him, how his headaches were killing him, his deep depression gnawing at everything. If we told the completeness of our stories to each other, who amongst us would come forward to our rescue?

■ In the dream we get into a taxi at a place that looks like the new Arts Centre in Tel Aviv. Gabriel says he needs to get some cash from the ATM, so we drop him off – it looks like Plaça de la Independència in Girona – and we keep driving, intending to pick him up later, but he's not there when we get back. I call his phone. Then I see him, his silhouette, drinking with a group of people, looking like something out of an ad for Coca Cola, young and animated. When I approach him he mumbles something in English – it's incoherent – and refuses to speak Hebrew (but he doesn't speak Hebrew, I think in the dream) and it's clear he has no intention of getting back into the taxi, but we keep driving round and round, expecting something to change.

Mundesley

&

■ The sound of water comes through the wall each time she moves in the tub. The woman in the room next door has a limp. She'd broken her leg a year ago while playing tennis, caught her foot in the grass and fell.

"And I remember thinking," she'd said to Gertler. "As I was falling, this thought that... my leg is breaking."

The last time he was here, Unwin had been bedridden, heart and stomach eaten away by the bug. Gertler had sat by his bedside. It took him all year to die in that cold month of Gertler's birthday. A card from Turner in London, a.teasing PS to remind him – ha, ha, so funny – that the artist at thirty-five will have exhausted his muse, leaving only the repetition of old themes and techniques.

And a happy birthday to you, too.

This time he'd arrived a leper, coughed out of society, unfit for human interaction, punished for something, his betrayal of the past, years of poverty and struggle – being squeezed and constricted. He'd have to hang himself, slit his wrists, cut off his hands – find a way to stop painting, to stop life.

Stop being ridiculous!

But it's spring. Garsington all over again.

He turns on the bedside lamp and scribbles a letter to his brother: I'm not fit enough to write, but I'm making progress. I can walk fifty yards. They follow me day and night in case I kill myself. I hate being washed by the nurse and helped to the pot. I shit in front of her. As for my mental side, I wonder if I'll ever paint again. I shall never have the strength to get back to it. Inside me there is too much unhappiness. We need a little joy in our lives! I'm sorry to hear that you, too, are unwell. I hope your health improves. You must make an effort. Try and eat well. Food is good for the nerves.

The dawn moon turns the edges of the leaves to silver. His hunger for beauty grows. When it fades, as it often does, nothing can rescue him where once even the slightest thing could keep him from falling. He needs familiar faces, to have a reason to return to his canvas. He thinks of the window back in his studio, close to the Heath. Hours in one place. Grief clouds his imagination. Grief for himself and for everything he has worked for – recognition, self-reliance, neither of which have come to him. So he creeps away from the sanatorium, across the dewy lawn, heading for the woods.

■ We drive up the coast to Sheringham, then Cromer, and walk along the prom, further up past the caravan park laid out like a refugee camp. You would think this was the edge of the world. Back in the car, we drive and chat – idle, comfortable talk – until the turnoff to Mundesley, pausing at the top of the hill, the sanatorium down below in the valley at the end of a winding road.

I imagine Marjorie at the door to his room, daffodils in hand, watching, a blanket up to his neck, a cup of tea, steam rising as if to clear his lungs, a slice of Victoria sponge on a saucer by his bedside. She gently taps the doorframe.

"How are you this morning?"

"Damned awful," he says, trying hard not to flinch.

"I'm sorry to hear that," she says.

"You could have waited till I looked up," he says. "I was just enjoying a spot of peace and quiet."

"Should I go?" she says.

He says nothing.

Marjorie pulls the armchair closer to his bed. The room is spacious and light, windows up to the ceiling, looking out onto sky and treetops. The embroidered cushions are puffed up and neatly arranged along the window seat.

"Thank you for coming," he says.

She takes his hand and brings it to her lips.

"You're cold," she says.

"It seems incredible that I shall ever be on my feet again."

He hands her the tea cup, folds his arms across his chest.

"When you're out, we'll head back to France," she says. "It'll do you good to get away."

"I'm already away," he says. "This place is away."

"Mister Gertler," a nurse knocks, her tone efficient. "We'll have to ask Mrs Gertler to leave us for a moment. The bandages need changing."

The sanatorium is now a drug rehabilitation centre. We should check with reception, tell them we're here – I'm writing a book about... I'd be grateful if... Starlings and robins bob in and out of a birdhouse near the picnic table, a grasshopper lands just in front of us, skinny legs bent back like the top part of a triangle, ready to jump.

"I'd move here in a heartbeat," Gabriel says.

The noise beneath his window is scrawny animals at each other's throats, screeching over raw meat. He waits until... quiet. Then it starts again, killing the sadness and the softness of his soul, talons begin to appear – horns, scales on the back of his hands, everywhere – and he craves flesh to grip in his teeth, hurl across the room, warm blood on his chin. What if he dies now, what will he be known for? And this rage... this little life, penniless, always waiting, the illusion that there is time, that the break will come. The break that happened twenty years ago, then went, and what good did it do? Don't give fame to the young – it cuts short one's life-span and relevance. There is no time to start again.

"Mark," she says.

Out on the lawn the track is marked with lime and cordoned off by ropes and stakes, it's the egg-and-spoon race, staff versus patients, guests cheering from the sidelines, or, like him and Marjorie, from the window-seat in their rooms.

"Let's walk in the back garden," he says.

"Do you feel strong enough?" she says.

"It'll be quieter there," he says.

All I seem to do, he thinks, is walk short distances then fall over. Like a wind-up doll. There is no solution... after all these years painting with my blood. It's not enough to say never mind the results. The important thing for a painter is to paint. I am tired of tests and temperatures. A yellow rose bush grows beside their bench. I have my thorns, too. The underside of each leaf a pale version of the dark flipside, thorns brown and red, flat at the bottom and curving up like waves. He snaps off a thorn, thinks about cleaning his nails, picking food – was there any? – from between his teeth. The petals a mixture of yellow and dark pink, as veiny as the leaves, almost red at the tips. Small fern-like leaves cup the bud. Trace the lines of my ribs, count them like treasures, fingertips to the hip bone, the pelvis.

"I wasn't always like this," he says, pressing petals between thumb and index finger, extracting their scent.

"I know," she says.

"You think I'm gentle and kind," he says.

The more it opens, the more beautiful it gets, petals leaning back to release music, romantic dreams. But his mind remains fixed to its essence, afraid to unravel.

"We're not flower people," he says.

"I do like tulips and daffodils," she says.

"We're peasant stock. Dealers in animal hide."

Happier with awls and creasing tools. But there was Ottoline's garden, the rockery by the pond, lawns, fruit trees, a mass of hydrangeas. His life far from the East End, from home, hopping between islands of beauty, brief reprieves, havens of salvation and denial, and between and around them all: poverty and apprehension. Marjorie sits with her hands in her lap, those hands that have touched him everywhere and not once recoiled.

"I feel proud to have a wife like you."

"Why do you say that?"

"It's true."

"You're very kind," she says.

"I'm getting better," he says. "We'll be in Paris soon."

"We will," she says. "Yes," she says. "We will be."

He snaps a bud off the rose bush and puts it in his

pocket. Back in his room he will open the petals, pull them back one by one to lean against his palm, a child resting its head on a pillow.

A young man walks along the edges of the lawn and slows down when he sees us. I imagine he'll ask for drugs, a cigarette, get us to smuggle something out, talk us into buying vodka from the off-license in Cromer. But he sits with us – *Who are you visiting again?* – and is more interested in his cigarette than in conversation, every so often checking to see how much is left, flicking his ash onto the grass, a hint of disappointment each time, and then, with his final puff, as if this has all been planned, we get up and go to his room.

"I'd rather watch," Gabriel says.

"Yeah," the guy says. "Keep an eye. The fucking Gestapo are out there."

He has baby fat under his T-shirt, pert little nipples, skin as smooth as a teenager's – when did I ever have skin like that? – and his breath is sweet and fresh, a taste I remember from long ago, a mixture of chewing gum and nicotine. He presents his body before us, naked, a thick bush of pubic hair, his cock fat and erect. It's been a while, he shrugs. A look of desperation, but a confidence in his beauty. *Fuck*, he says, and pulls my face to his, his lips soft and fleshy, his tongue pressing into my mouth. *Come on, man*, he says to Gabriel. *Let me feel you.* But

Gabriel has his back to us and stays put. *I'm alright*, he says. *You two go ahead.*

I want to remember Gertler the way you'd want to remember the dead, the sound of them, details of their days, time spent together, all to ensure their return at unexpected moments, visitations, reminders that the past is here, that we've not forgotten. In the relinquishing of all scruples, of anything that matters, in the soft body supple with boredom and passivity, long days trapped in bed, Gertler's story grafts itself onto my memory, my life fusing with his, this possible version of an artist's trajectory. It's not just my cock the guy wants inside him, not just my fingers, he wants everything, an insatiable hunger for life, to be consumed, filled, to disappear and become, to un-separate, never just him and the thing that eats away at him from inside.

Don't, I think. Not death. And I whisper it into his ear as I'm about to come: "I won't let you," I say. "I won't."

"What?" he says. "What, baby?"

"I won't," I say. "I won't. I won't."

All echoes are drowned out by the eagerness of sex, by the clamour and urgency and wonder of a new body, memories of others, bodies we've been drawn to, going back and back to the first, the one that made it possible for us to forget who we were, in all that – *that knoll of plumage* – for a short while there was only skin and breath.

Gabriel walks across the room to sit on the side of the bed, a hand on my back, stroking, the warmth of him.

"That feels nice," I say.

"What are we doing?" he says.

"This is fucked up," I say.

"Let's go," he says. "We're done with Gertler. We've got Paris to pack for."

■ "And when I die," Gertler says. "Who'll be sad?"

"Stop," she says. "You're getting better."

"I'm dying."

"You're going home in a couple of days."

"Katherine's dead. Carrington's dead. My mother's dead. And now…"

They finish their tea in silence.

Never underestimate people's desire to live, nor assume this is the last goodbye. How will it end? In this room in Mundesley looking out the window, scabs forming on his skin, washed and wiped by nurses. Over the next few days the daffodils will bow their heads, then begin to open. He will see the symbolism in that – we open to the world after we've been at our most humble – and he'll allow himself, as he drifts into sleep, a momentary flicker of hope.

■ I will take you to the graves in the old town where the Arabs used to live (as if *enough*, they said, and packed

Mark

their bags), to the shop in the market where we'd go for Iraqi pita bread, as big as dinner plates, warm from the oven, covered in chocolate spread then rolled up to eat. I will take you to the sea. That is where we must go, back to the sea, to the empty stretch of beach: long runs and night swimming, dunes, shrubs, the Sheik's tomb at the top of the cliff where we'd sit at night and smoke and make out with girls.

If we go back.

This is how I imagine it. We will stay in my sister's place in Ashkelon, the flat I grew up in, the flat she moved into after our mother's death, then out again when the rockets from Gaza became too much. In the distance we will hear the bombings, rockets landing on the outskirts of the town, but we're safe. It'll be a warm night and dinner will be over and we'll have done the dishes and I'm upstairs in my father's roof garden, a cool breeze from the sea and the sky bright with the moon turning the bougainvillea purple. I'm looking into the neighbour's bathroom window, the way I did when I was a boy, watching him shower, getting ready for bed. I was in my last year of high school when he shot himself one afternoon in the middle of the week. His wife found him dead in the bathroom.

I imagine you and I climbing down the eight floors and walking along the back roads towards the beach. Sometimes you're with me, and I feel the thrill of showing you my world, where I'm from, this route I took most days after school, escaping from home to spend hours on the beach, often until sunset. Or you're asleep in the flat and I'm out here alone, the streets deserted. It's early morning and the town is mine. I walk across the dunes towards the shore, towards the music of the waves, the soothing monotony of water falling onto water, especially in the dark, a sound that drowns out all other sounds, a sound that calms and soothes, crashing and crashing and crashing.

Paris

෮

■ *The good thing about being here*, Gertler thinks, as he gets ready for bed, his last night at the sanatorium before heading back to London, then Paris – at last – *the good thing is the steady light.* This room to which he'll one day return and where he will slit his wrists and cut his throat but not yet die, *I've had my materials, everything I've needed.* The word shone before him – Paris – wide streets, markets, long walks before lunch, the Louvre, Musée d'Orsay, anywhere for a Renoir. How the sun had shone that day, exposed until it set, the entire city open to him. In the middle of the *pont* Marie, look this way, that way, across Paris, the trees and vast sky, roads and cars, horses and carriages moving with and against the river's flow and he so happy, exultant, everything as one, him and the world.

He heads back towards boulevard Raspail, past the *triperie*, pheasants at the butcher's stall, beaks open, ribbons of blood trickling down the glass. The lady

139

butcher hacking at a pig. Rabbits on their backs, skinned and sliced open, locals gathering to select ingredients for dinner: vegetables, squash, peppers, a pomegranate.

He stands at the door to La Rotonde. A table of older women, *les dames* who'd left their apartments on rue de Rennes to *prend un verre*, in matching skirts and jackets, gold earrings – they, in particular, like to hear from the waiters about girlfriends or the health of their mothers. *How did the knee operation go?* Laughing at something the waiter says, flirting, because the waiter, too, likes to make a woman, any woman, but especially an older woman... likes to make her laugh, and Gertler smiles and waves across the room to where the Huxleys are sitting – *I didn't mean to be late* – and settles in for an afternoon of vermouth and macaroons.

■ When the body explodes, when the body of a man is detonated, part of its mass is released in the form of energy made of substances so miniscule there is no instrument to identify them. Mainly, there are chunks of gut and limb, rib and hair – and from the head: bone and brains and fragments of scull. An arm into this tree, a torso on the side of a road, a leg on the other, flesh and intestine plastered to cement blocks that lead to the gate where I stand. One minute a man is walking towards you, hands outstretched, waving a double hello – *hello, hello* – the next there is blood on your cheeks, your uniform. You freeze, I froze, stunned, my mind racing between surrender and howling. Then you open fire, I opened fire, just from the shock, a tin soldier, petrified, rigid, emptying an entire magazine onto the spot where the man had been, where his body had exploded.

Later they will tell me how I screamed, that I sounded like a wild and wounded animal. That they stood and watched, then took me back to the tent, gave me sleeping pills and I slept. In the evening, they retold how they'd gathered the body parts so that when soldiers from the battalion headquarters came to pick them up, pieces of the man would be ready in plastic bags.

■ "I remember the light," I say to Gabriel. "The pure bright yellow that came from him, the explosion from his own body illuminating its fragmentation. That's what I thought afterwards. Like he wanted to be sure I saw everything. First he was a person coming towards me, then, just like that, he was gone."

I know we are not alone. I know this is a café in Paris, me and this man I am beginning to love. I know there are people at the tables around us, cutlery clinking, mussel shells ripped open, cups of coffee lifted to lips and lips pursing to sip. I am here with Gabriel, but I am somewhere else, too, caught up in this desperate articulation of history, its weight, my skin, a calcified layer of memory hardening over everything.

"I remember shouting '*Qui êtes-vous?*' but he never said anything. Then the boom and the exploding light."

Gabriel leans closer, comes towards me, and I want to tell him to stay where he is, but I say nothing and I am quiet and he takes my hand.

"Let me tell you..." – but by now I am sobbing, and this awful sadness and guilt, to say and not fall apart, to begin to feel what it would be like to kneel before this story and howl like a dog. To vomit it out of myself, as if I could be purged, as if I could turn myself inside out. As if this shell of memory could crack.

"You can't let go now," I say.

"I need you, too," he says.

"This will always be with us."

"Yes," Gabriel says. "I know." He says: "I know."

■ In the morning, Gertler waits in the vestibule watching porn flicks. The young boy across from him sits with his eyes glued to the flickering screen, hands in lap, fingers wound tightly, the large arm of his uncle around his shoulder. They sit and watch in silence, waiting their turn while on the screen a man with a bushy moustache propositions a woman reading a book on a bench by the Seine. He takes her to a hotel nearby, and immediately she lies down, lifts her skirt and goes down on her, hungrily.

When Gertler finally goes in, the woman is Tunisian,

around thirty. Beautiful. Jewish. *All the whores in this city*, someone had said, *are Jews*. He loves the way she wraps herself around him, draws him in, her body softer and larger, so for a moment, with his eyes closed, for just a second, she is someone else. Afterwards, they lie in silence and smoke until she gets up, sits on the edge of the bed (always a back turned) and coughs a wad of phlegm into her handkerchief like an oyster of blood.

Later, years later, or perhaps on the same visit (who can remember?) him and Marjorie sat by the river on a bench opposite l'Orangerie. Chestnuts in blossom, the smell of thick white petals, close together (just yesterday they were married) as an omnibus moves along the opposite bank towards the Hôtel-Dieu like a duck at a playground shooting-range. *A bus like a duck, chuck.* The French flag on a barge sways in the wind. Behind them, midday strollers and cars and carriages, all from left to right, right to left, lines on a page, everything a sentence – some English, some Yiddish – back and forth. Only the ducks and seagulls unfettered by the page, neither intention nor obligation to fly with the river's course, towards Dieppe, Calais, the sea, home. People cross bridges, top to bottom, from the bottom up. If the world was a page... if the world... and the page would be yes, lined against chaos. The page is canvas. Ink is oil. The page is mirror. The pen – shadow.

On their walk back to the hotel on rue des Beaux Arts, they chance upon a gallery with a Liebermann exhibition, that grand painting of Samson and Delilah, a biblical story stripped bare. Gertler imagines Abraham and Isaac, Lot and his daughters, Solomon and the Queen of Sheba. Yael and Sisra. Hagar on the night her son was conceived. Reducing each story to its essence, no abstraction, no landscape, just a bed, rumpled sheets, a triumphant Delilah holding aloft her lover's ponytail.

Quick! One last look at the Cezannes in the Pellerin Collection: *Battle of Love*, *Modern Olympia*. Renoirs... their impression – enormous, following his brushstrokes, exquisite, refined, the desire for brutality, something less precious, bolder. He's desperate to get back to work. Paris always changes him. It's where he became a painter, not just to paint – he'd been doing that forever – but *to be* a painter. To live that life, to go out into the world and be that. Big cities give us that, it's where we can be writers or painters, philosophers, where we don't have to worry about people coming to visit, events to attend, mundane obligations. They allow us to exclude our other selves, to forge... to forget.

■ We unlock a couple of *velibs* from a docking station on Boulevard du Montparnasse and cycle the long way back towards our hotel in the 16th, up Boulevard Saint-Michel and across the river to Boulevard de Sebastopol, then left onto Rue de Rivoli, late-night traffic flowing to our left, then along the edges of Place de la Concorde, past the American Embassy, the tree-lined street quiet at this time of night, gendarmes talking to each other from either side of the road. It's almost midnight, April in Paris, 2009. America has a new president, swine flu is spreading in Mexico, the Gazans are in shock, bush fires rage across Australia, the Taliban have beheaded a Polish geologist, an earthquake has killed hundreds in Italy, and in Peru, Fujimora is on his way to prison.

"I still want to go," Gabriel says.

"Where?"

"You know where."

"Will you come with me?" I say.

"Of course I will," he says.

"And hold my hand?"

"Always," he says.

"Show me," and I reach out to him and he cycles up alongside me and takes my hand and we continue like this, holding hands, side-by-side, riding along the canopied avenue until we get to the junction with Avenue de Marigny and head left towards the Champs-Élysées. Who cares if it's hyperbole? There are words we need to hear, regardless of their resilience, no matter – but for that moment, the moment in which they are said, they are precisely what we want to hear.

I will hold your hand.

Always.

"Let's stop," I say.

"For what?" he says.

"I'm not sure," I say. "For this moment. To make it last."

London IV

ॐ

■ It's hard to work his way back to her. They're in the kitchen drinking tea. Gertler feels a recrimination coming on – and pity... he's a person to feel sorry for. He withdraws, folds in on himself, feels hounded. It's November 1931. They've been to Paris, got married. The honeymoon is over. The great depression is everywhere. Food is scarce. In the harbours, no goods to export, ships are rusting. From everywhere, hunger marches are descending on London. In America, drought has hit the Midwest, food prices are rising. The Panama Canal has been shut for weeks because of earthquakes. Ike Turner is born, Boris Yeltsin and James Dean are in nappies, Al Capone is going down for eleven years. In France, the police are closing in on the Corsican bandits. The Nazi Party's gaining power. Hitler's sorting out his papers to become a German citizen. Mao proclaims the Chinese Soviet Republic while the Huang He floods kill millions.

And now for the good news: The Empire State

Building is ready, gambling's made legal in Vegas, *Frankenstein* and *Mata Hari* are showing at the pictures. Progress is at hand: nylon, the aerosol can, the electric razor have just been invented. A house in London costs £600, but if you wait a while, the prices will drop.

Nothing is more important to him than her happiness, to lift her from this gloom, make their union the thing to sustain them.

"I *do* want to give you a child," he says.

"What you want," she says, "excludes children."

"What you crave is selfish and naïve," she says.

"It's not selfishness," he says. "It's direction. I will not be spineless jelly. I will create things – paintings, life, this – with an inner vertebrae of purpose."

Stop.

No more.

Come closer.

His head on the kitchen table. She strokes his hair and he longs to be lifted and carried to bed, the way she's always done, pressing him to her chest, offering herself as food. He has never known such tenderness, as they kiss and whisper back and forth: *I love you. No more sadness.* Breathe, inhale. Whatever has come before, breathe it out.

■ One of us here at his desk, the other on his way home from a *Superman* matinée. My Gabriel is Superman, he who flies. Nimble and streamlined, his skin as smooth as feathers. I sit and write, barely moving, hair growing from every follicle like roots, as if air were earth.

Earlier today, the men in the swimming pool at the gym had been particularly beautiful. I love those days when the pool is full of them, diving into the water, backs gleaming like dolphins, slipping through my fingers. You can smell them underwater, those men who swim tirelessly back and forth. Water is a caul that transforms all of us into sublime creatures. I turn my head each time to breathe, each time to catch a glimpse of skin, the seaweed-lace in armpits, to punish myself for envy, this desire to possess and consume, to make my own, sinking to the bottom to wash my mouth out with chlorine. I have swallowed an entire pool and now I wait, chubby with pride, for Gabriel to return from the movies, for him to walk towards me, brimming with glee and waving his fingers playfully, threatening to tickle me.

■ Marjorie stopped painting so he could paint (painting was his domain and executioner), covered her drawings, made them face the wall. By the end, she was tiptoeing around him, coming home to prepare food, keeping out of his way. At least with the house to himself he was free to paint, free from the push-me-pull-you of devotion and evasion. For months, his only thought had been: I want a year of bachelorhood. This perpetual dread chips away at hope, gnawing relentlessly. A desire to be undomesticated. Whatever I make goes into paying debts. I owe more money than I will ever make.

He'd tried to warn her that this sadness would never leave him. It was bigger than him, bigger than the two of them put together, an exquisite sadness, a despair to keep revisiting, nostalgia for the tumult of childhood, its insecurity and deprivation. His torment – an acting out of the secret of poverty – a resounding "no" to everything, and in the end, to life.

By the time it was all over between them, Marjorie was in one room and he in another. If she was having an affair, it was happening between meal times. Sometimes she'd prepare lunch in the mornings and leave instructions: EAT OR HEAT. They hardly spoke, not even at the dinner table, those times when she was at home and he was at home and they'd eat together. Those evenings were the worst, this miserable quagmire they'd got themselves into. She read a novel and thought about god knows what, he shovelled food down with a rage that was ugly even to himself.

"This is good," he said, pointing with his fork to his egg and sausages.

"Good," she said.

The deep unrest between them had killed everything and he didn't want to fix it, didn't want the domestic banality of it all. Oh, he could go on and on about what was wrong, but the *unteste shureh* is... he wants to be alone. He was always like that, and he dreams of going back to that time, to the sweet melancholy loneliness of his studio on Elder Street, seeing no one for days, Dostoyevsky in the evenings, afternoon walks along the Embankment, then working so hard all you ever saw of him was his ghost.

■ Soon I'll be leaving for the Holyland. I mean, *we'll* be leaving. Almost fifteen years since you and I were together there. I'm coming back to finish this book I've been writing for the past few years. I thought I'd never return to the place that makes me feel so much shame and regret. Even naming it marks it, drags my narrative down like a dead weight. I have distanced myself, and perhaps I've never felt that it was mine, but it is the place, as they say, that begat me. I grew up there, had a mother and father, a sister (you), a home, schooling, survived the wars. But my people are not from there. Jews are not from anywhere. Having spent the past fifteen years in the diaspora, I am sure of that.

I know, I know... you hate London. After your time here you said you wanted nothing more to do with the English. You'd never met a breed of people so rude. Savages. The words they get right, but their tone is vile. They try to pass themselves off as civilised.

I'm not sure why I'm coming back. My new man

wants to see, and I want to stop being so scared. You and I have never talked about what happened – nobody ever does – as if there is some tacit agreement that those of us who didn't kill or shoot anyone, have nothing to say, that what we went through doesn't count. The ones who should be silent, who should be suppressing memories (or confessing), who have things to hide, are those who were on the front-line and did what people do on front-lines. They are running the country. But there is more to it than that.

■ Gabriel comes home with sunflowers and sets up his easel in the living room. This is the first time he has painted here and I sit quietly on the sofa, as if one wrong move could disrupt his private ritual. He opens the window onto the street, then stands still for a moment, absorbing, the occasional woosh of a car or bus. He sketches first: the flowers in the vase – pencil marks across a page – and the window frame, the night sky. Then he prepares a palette – indigo, yellow ochre, white, purple madder – and begins to put what's out there onto the canvas, intent, frowning – and I think of the word "capture," what it means to see something, out there or in your head, and to translate it, feel compelled to, as if translation makes the world, as if the world relies on transformation to stop itself from reverting to chaos – inside the colours, ingesting the sunflowers, the sky, the window, remaking them on the canvas, the yellow, the white, the green. And when it's done, when it will be done, when it's ready, hours from now, days, he will hand it to me... this is what we must appreciate, as if to say, as if to say this, this is what I have made of the world.

From the street below, a group of football fans drags us away from the moment, back to this room, back to time, routine, sleep. Gabriel turns to me. "Okay," he says. "I'm exhausted," and laughs and plonks himself down on the sofa beside me, his arm warm against mine, his head on my shoulder, a small child, returning.

"Time for bed," he says.

"I'll make cocoa," I say. "Go clean your brushes."

■ Celia had been sitting for him since early morning, the glass doors open onto the garden. He gets distracted, his mind wanders, a cat jumps from the wall onto the patio and stops to regard him. Where are you off to? His hand's becoming comfortable again, everything's starting to fit as he draws, ready to pick up the brush, to take what's in front of him and apply it to the canvas, dots of pink, purple, pin-pricks of red, yellow, orange. Celia shifts in her chair, jolts him away from his work, back to this house (soon to be sold), his deteriorating condition, back to the strict routine of walks on the Heath, regular meals, his longing for other women, frustration at not having sold anything at the Lefevre exhibition

Leave the painting and walk in the garden, but he promised himself to keep going until one, until the sun was past its peak. Each brush-stroke an attempt to rise from the ground. The stories of childhood, petty squabbles, the Great Move, then back to London, then the War... all this must be eked from the bristles of his paintbrush. It was up to him to shave colours off stone, blend dust with oil: from earth to canvas – to generate every step, to squeeze paint from tubes like excrement, colours from his own flesh. History was creeping up on him, the war that will wipe out his people. The next few years will mark the end of decency.

I want to offer my soul naked to the world so that for a single second it will explode into flames.

Hitler's speech resounds... no one will help us if we don't help ourselves... this is a manly pursuit, this fortifying of Germany, better than begging from all and sundry... his attack on England, war's inevitable, and when it does break out Gertler knows they'll close the school where he teaches, stop the salaries. The familiar crisis begins to close in on him, the depression that makes it all unbearable, worry interrupts every thought and desire. All I'm trying to do is create things of beauty. How else can he handle the anger that lurks beneath the surface, ready to emerge as an all-consuming blaze. Welling up in his throat, turning thick in his mouth. He spits into a handkerchief. The poison is him.

He kneels to peel rose madder from the floor, the soothing ache as a shard of dried colour digs under his fingernail. I could go through them all, he thinks – titanium, raw umber, vermilion, yellow – every wafer of paint slicing into me. His whole body without outline, as if he could spill out of himself, turn liquid, splatter on the floor, be the overspill. Just when he thinks he can breathe again, when he's beginning to think the world is expanding, something comes along to make him feel spent – a letter from the Jewish Education Aid Society to remind him he still owes £80 from thirty years ago. Every noise distracts, denies him the isolation he needs, and he hates the weather, the dark skies, the relentless showers.

Write a farewell note, explain, but whatever he says will leave someone with guilt – there's no way to save them from feeling they could have done more, because they could have – bought more paintings, loved him, devoted their lives to him. And some of them – you know who you are – could have stayed alive rather than set bad examples. This was not going to be another note he'd write to himself then tear up and burn.

■ I imagine sunlight between dark narrow streets. I imagine his teacher from Deal Street School, Miss Macintosh, on her way home in the late afternoon, pausing at the junction of Middlesex Street and Bishopsgate, warm in the sunshine, a pond of light, the fabric of her skirt thick and comforting. She's almost forty, alone for the past fifteen years. There's never been a man in her life – no lover, no father, her brothers left years ago for Africa – no man since the one who changed his mind and immigrated to Australia. She hates the thought of travel, being stuck on a boat. It makes her nauseous just to think of it.

She'll put the painting on the wall.

"For you, miss," he'd said, handing her the sheet of paper laid flat in his open palms. And once she'd taken it, he kept standing there, as if expecting something in return.

A bowl of apples.

There in the light – yes, like an apple in a bowl, sunshine on her cheeks, facing Smith's Dining Rooms, almost ready to cross the road with its horse-drawn carriages, an omnibus with stairs helter-skelter up to the top deck. She is in the moment, all attachments relinquished, happy to notice how happy she is, to be here at this point in time, a single woman, independent, bringing good to the East End, glad to be amongst them, amongst the boys in their suits and bibs, their Sunday best all week, and the girls with their large white ribbons tied high on their heads, sleeves puffed up like angel wings.

■ Later that day, when Celia returned to sit for him, she

called his name, then went around the back. He might be in his studio, though he always came to the door when she knocked. The thoughts as he fades are of summer, endless miles of beach, walking along the water's edge, the sun feeding his skin. He tries to think of painting, the doing of it, but even the thought of a completed picture brings him no pleasure, as if now, in this warm and all-engulfing sunshine, his work as a painter is done. She pushes against the door that pushes against the mattress that rocks him from side to side, the sun turning the calm sea silver and the water dazzles. Yes, that dark patch in the distance is a boat, or seaweed, or a gull, or the light playing tricks on water. She kneels beside him. He is naked, his clothes in a pile by the mattress – a pink shirt, a pale tie, a fawn-coloured suit – as if he'd undressed for bed. He is thin and soft, his skin warm. That first night he'd woken at the edge of the room on the floor beside his mother, the others asleep under sacks, and he'd cried quietly, so as not to wake them, his heart overcome with a gloom that would never leave. All he wants is a destination, to be driven by faith, a path along the hard sand, only inches from the waves. And the man at the gate says: "Where to?"

And he points in that direction. "There," he says.

The garden is in full bloom – the peonies and zinnias and delphiniums are wide open. Luke is in Davos getting stronger, turning brown on the shores of the lake, diving into cool water. Marjorie is drinking white wine and laughing with Franz (they've just made love), and Eddie is worrying about the war that's about to start. Celia puts her lips to Gertler's forehead and whispers something, but all he hears is the hissing of the gas and the chirping of evening birds.

■ People draw their blinds, shut their windows, stay indoors as if they lived in tents. Dust settles on everything, gets into everything, you swallow it on the way to work, on the beach, in a café, breathe it in, this reminder that we're in the desert, so much space and so little room to breathe, a reminder that any bit of green around you, no matter how close you are to the sea, will one day be covered.

It creeps up on me unexpectedly, now that we're in the air, now that we're on our way, the ambivalence about going is muted, it's a kind of relief, and I'm overtaken by anticipation. Somewhere, on some level, I want to slot back into my life, pick up where I left off, not that I can remember clearly where that was, fifteen years ago, in my early thirties, when the language I spoke was not the language I am writing in, but a language hauled back from the house of prayer and longing. And while we sit here, close together, Gabriel and I, our elbows touching as we eat our in-flight meal, I feel that finding him has changed me. There have been moments when this feeling of love has been like loss, as if to want and to lose are indistinguishable. There is the full spectrum: gratitude, wonder, indifference, joy, glee, dread, loss – always loss – and completeness, like nothing else is needed, nothing except his voice and his body close to mine – and, my god, how is that possible? How can it be that everything I have wished for is in this, in him, in our being together?

Maybe there'll be a gap between this visit and the next. I will tell the story and that's all I can do for now. Silence is worse. There are parts of me that Gabriel cannot know, that he does not know, and parts of him – family, childhood, lives lived before we met, enduring connections with others, other men, and also... so much...

"You're still a big puzzle," I say. "I've told you so much already."

"That doesn't mean I know you," he says.

"No," I say.

"And I'm glad for that," he says.

The plane begins its descent and my ears hurt with the pressure and I want the pain to consume me, for my body to be overwhelmed by it, the stabbing in my ears, this searing pain and this fear in my gut, and I will give myself over to it. I will be only pain and evacuation and sealing up, running and the turning to stone, drama and boredom, silence and racket, the hunting and the sleeping, breathing into each other's mouths, the light and shade, darkness and fireworks, hope and cessation.

And for a moment I think this is familiar, that I've done this before, that this is repetition – but it's not, because you take my hand, Gabriel, you take my hand as we get closer to the runway – and there is none of the dread, none of the horror, and as we land I think: this is new, this is something I have not done before. We are, you and I, only at the beginning, and the beginning with you is a sight for sore eyes.

Printed in Poland
by Amazon Fulfillment
Poland Sp. z o.o., Wrocław